"Is there a safehouse?" asked Dirty Shirt.

Gerber grimaced. "'Fraid not. We're having a hell of a time keeping indigenous agents alive in the North. The only logistical support we'll have will be what we carry in on our backs. Naturally we can radio the SFOB and requisition items for airdrop. But if we do have to resort to that, we'll run the risk of detection when we key the transmitter. Their intercept operators might pick up our broadcast on a routine frequency sweep. We wouldn't want that."

Bocker joined in on the conversation. "Well, we've got to have commo with the SFOB to coordinate extraction. We're bringing a CW burst device to cut down the length of transmission time. Odds are they'll never even hear us on the air."

Gerber's face took on a stern demeanor and his voice was very sober. "There's something we need to talk about. If anyone is captured, talk. Tell them anything. Lie, or tell the truth. Either way it doesn't matter. Because if anyone is caught, we're going to assume the worst—that you've talked and compromised the mission. Do whatever you need to do to minimize the torture, the pain. It's your call."

Also available by Eric Helm:

VIETNAM: GROUND ZERO
P.O.W.
UNCONFIRMED KILL
THE FALL OF CAMP A-555
SOLDIER'S MEDAL
THE KIT CARSON SCOUT
THE HOBO WOODS
GUIDELINES
THE VILLE
INCIDENT AT PLEI SOI
TET
THE IRON TRIANGLE

VIETNAM: GROUND ZERO™.

RED DUST

ERIC HELM

A GOLD EAGLE BOOK FROM
WORLDWIDE®

TORONTO • NEW YORK • LONDON • PARIS
AMSTERDAM • STOCKHOLM • HAMBURG
ATHENS • MILAN • TOKYO • SYDNEY

First edition August 1988

ISBN 0-373-62713-0

VIETNAM: GROUND ZERO.™
RED DUST

Dedicated to Timothy P. Banse
without whose assistance and expertise
this book could not have been written.

PROLOGUE

KILLED IN ACTION
TRAVEL BUREAU
REPUBLIC OF SOUTH
VIETNAM, FEBRUARY 1
1968

Midnight found Army PFC James O'Hanlon on watch.
He was on one side of the horseshoe-shaped perimeter,
sitting in a two-man hole and eating C-rations. Next to
him Corporal Troy Billingsley slept on, his turn at guard
not scheduled to begin for another hour.

O'Hanlon was an FNG. He'd been in-country for a
week and in the bush for a day. A young man with red
hair, freckles and a mouth full of gleaming white teeth,
he was one of the youngest men in the army, having lied
about his age to a recruiter who was more interested in
filling quotas than in making sure that all the paperwork was legal.

The lieutenant had paired him with Billingsley, who
was about to rotate home. It was Billingsley who had told
him that the average GI participated in 10.5 firefights.
It was Billingsley who had confessed to O'Hanlon that

he, Billingsley, was always scared, but never thought of running.

"It's more dangerous to run," Billingsley had said. "If Charlie doesn't get you in the open, the lieutenant will."

"Wouldn't he let one man run?" O'Hanlon had asked.

"If he let one man, we'd all run."

The quick pad of feet on the road drew O'Hanlon's attention from his food and from his thoughts. He looked along the barrel of the M-60 machine gun and felt an icy hand grab his stomach. Billingsley hadn't told him what to do if someone approached from down the road. No one was supposed to be out there. He thought about waking the corporal, but didn't want to look like an asshole.

He sucked the white plastic spoon clean and slipped it into the top pocket of his jungle jacket as he'd seen the others do earlier. He glanced at Billingsley's sleeping form and then leaned his shoulder into the butt of the M-60.

A dim figure approached on the moon-dappled road. O'Hanlon took careful aim; at twenty yards he wasn't likely to miss. He began to take up the slack in the trigger, then hesitated.

Should he challenge? Should he shoot? It could be a friendly papa-san walking home from his fields. But at midnight?

O'Hanlon cranked back the bolt of the M-60, ejecting a live round, wanting the shadowy figure in front of him to hear the sound of the bullet chambering.

"Do not shoot," said a quiet voice from the darkness.

The voice sounded like that of a young boy, O'Hanlon noted as he raised his head over the sights of the M-60. "Friend or foe?"

"Friend, *Dai uy*. Do not shoot."

"What's the password?"

"I do not know, *monsieur*."

The shadowy figure was very close now. "You look VC. Get your hands in the air and walk toward me." O'Hanlon could feel his heart pounding in terror. A moment later a youth stood in front of O'Hanlon with his loose cotton shirt and trousers floating in the hot breeze.

"Turn around," barked O'Hanlon. He glanced to his right and saw that Billingsley was awake now and watching. The older man nodded once, as if approving O'Hanlon's handling of the situation.

The newcomer turned slowly, aware that a quick motion might spook the American soldier. O'Hanlon left his post, carrying his M-16. As he moved, Billingsley slipped behind the machine gun to provide cover.

O'Hanlon approached the stranger and began to search him, the barrel of his weapon touching the back of the boy's head. Starting at the ankle, he ran his hand up the inside of the right pant leg. That started a violent trembling and O'Hanlon was sure that the boy was armed. Roughly, he reached around the boy's chest looking for a concealed pistol or hand grenade. When his fingers brushed against the unmistakable protuberance of a woman's breast, he recoiled.

"My God, y-you're a girl," he stammered.

"*Oui, monsieur*. A girl."

O'Hanlon stepped back. He could see her better now. The young woman stood about five foot two. She was a lithe creature with long, straight black hair and a slight curve to her back. "What in Buddha's name are you doing sneaking around in the boonies after midnight?"

"I wanted to contact the Americans," she replied, speaking very good English. The slightly built girl looked about sixteen years old.

"Why? What do you want?"

"Food," she said. "My parents are dead. My little sister and I are hungry. We want something to eat." Her face twitched as if she was about to burst into tears. "I have no money."

O'Hanlon nodded. "What's your name?"

"Thuy Thien," she said shyly, bowing her head slightly.

"I'll see if I can scrounge something for you to eat." He pointed to the ground behind his foxhole. "Sit. Don't move a muscle."

He stepped down into his hole, rummaged around in his pack and came away with two boxes of C-rations. Before he could hand them to her, Billingsley grabbed his arm.

"What the fuck are you doing?"

"I'm giving her something to eat."

"Right. Shit." He stared up at O'Hanlon. "Just don't get carried away."

O'Hanlon turned and handed the rations to the girl. She took one and opened it.

O'Hanlon felt overcome by a strong sexual desire. He knelt on the ground in front of her and began to unfasten her blouse one button at a time. His veins were full of fire, first from nearly loosing a burst from the M-60 and now at the prospect of the joy that was about to happen.

Shoulders held high, Thuy Thien began to cry.

O'Hanlon had run into this once before, in the back seat of his '57 Chevy the night before he had been shipped overseas. He had felt like a fool ever since over the missed opportunity. Tears or not, he was determined not to let the Vietnamese girl interfere with his pleasure.

"Why are you crying?" he asked, fumbling with the last button.

"I am a virgin," she said in a very quiet voice.

He let go of her blouse. "A virgin?"

"Oui," she whispered back.

O'Hanlon was silent for a moment. "Jesus. Why me?" Then he got to his feet and turned his back on her. "Get dressed," he said quietly.

With her blouse hanging open to her tiny waist, she stared longingly at the cardboard boxes full of food.

"They're yours," he said curtly. "Just take the Cs and go. Goodbye."

Tears streaked her dusty face as she slowly refastened the buttons. She stared at his name tag for a moment as if she were reading it, then kissed him lightly on the cheek. She started back down the road from where she'd come.

From a few meters out she yelled back to him, "O'Hanlon, you are numbah one GI."

Billingsley looked at O'Hanlon as he dropped back into the hole. "O'Hanlon, you are number one dumb shit."

IF IT HAD BEEN a clear night, O'Hanlon could have seen the creeping, crawling NVA troops silhouetted alongside the dark tanks. Clad in khakis and webgear, the well-equipped regulars moved as silently as ghosts. But from the top of the hill, the suddenly wide-awake soldiers of Alpha Company could only hear the ominous clanking of the tracked armor coming at them.

The RTO asked the CO, "You want to call one of the fire support bases for illuminating rounds?"

The CO shook his head. "No good. We're not in their zone."

"Can't be our tanks out there. All the armored units have orders not to move at night," offered the RTO nervously.

"You never know. There are always exceptions. We'll just have to wait and see."

Finally, through the lenses of the hand-held Starlite scope the CO saw the ghostly green shapes running across the gray fog. The major fastened his flak jacket and then popped a flare, illuminating the sky with burning daylight. When he saw the black pajamas, Billingsley set off the claymore mine. The detonation hurled a wall of steel ball bearings at the enemy, cutting down a dozen of the attackers. He followed up with a series of short bursts from the M-60, tracking the blistering fire as close to the ground as possible.

Charlie came yelling in the night. On either side of Billingsley, M-16s on full-auto clattered in nervous hands. The air smelled of burned gunpowder and hot brass. Hundreds of rifles and machine guns seemed to be firing at once. Some of the attackers went down suddenly. But the bullets didn't stop the tanks or the soldiers who had dodged behind them for cover.

The major slithered alongside Billingsley and started babbling in an excited voice. "We'd better make a run for it, we can't hold 'em off. There're too many of them, we'll be overrun."

They ducked as an RPG whooshed over their heads and slammed into the ground behind them. It detonated in a burst of white heat. An American soldier screamed in agony. "I'm hit. I'm hit."

Billingsley never looked away from the gun sights. "Go ahead," he said to the major as he fired a long burst. "I can give you covering fire for a few more minutes." Billingsley's father had once told him that you could smell fear on a man. At the time Billingsley had no idea what that meant, but now with the odor of the major drifting into his nostrils he knew.

"I'll meet you back at the LZ, son." The major passed down the order to pull back and then he worked his way toward the RTO. "Head for the LZ. Get the choppers in here," he barked to the radioman.

Bent low, the nineteen-year-old blond soldier with the AN/PRC-25 radio strapped onto his back talked calmly and clearly into the microphone. "Easy Money, Easy Money, this is Alpha One, over."

The field radio crackled back, "Alpha One, this is Easy Money, over."

"Easy Money, this is Alpha One. We're taking fire, one US soldier legs are off, request dustoff. Grid coordinates follow...."

Interrupting the transmission, the major grabbed the mike from the RTO and screamed in a shrill voice, "Get that damn chopper!" He threw the mike at the radioman, and without thinking, stood to run. As if to chastise him, a giant hand thumped him in the chest. He did a double flip and landed flat on his back. Stunned by the impact, he got up clutching his chest, took a couple of tottering steps and collapsed to his knees. A big grin spread across his face as he realized he was still breathing because his flak jacket had saved his life.

The noise of the tanks grew louder as the rest of the company picked their way down the reverse slope of the hill and slipped into the tree line. One American soldier sprinting for the LZ stepped on a punji stake. Its razor-sharp point stabbed clear through his foot and poked out the top of the boot; he hadn't been issued the new jungle boots with the steel-sole insert. The punji anchor yanked him to a halt and he fell flat on his face, driving another stake through the palm of his hand.

Amid the noise of battle O'Hanlon heard an object hit the ground not far behind them. "Grenade," he screamed, curling up into a protective ball. Billingsley smacked the top of O'Hanlon's helmet. "Rocks, you idiot. They're throwing rocks to make you lose your cool." His composure regained, a chagrined O'Hanlon got back into position beside Billingsley.

Covering Alpha Company's strategic withdrawal, O'Hanlon fed belts of .30 caliber ammunition, while Billingsley fired them away. One after another, NVA soldiers stumbled and fell under the hail of ruby-red tracer and copper-jacketed ammunition. Over the clamor of the gun, Billingsley shouted, "None of my business, but how old are you, kid?"

"Nineteen," replied O'Hanlon.

"No, the truth," said Billingsley. O'Hanlon had lied to get in, and everyone in the unit knew it but had figured it was the kid's business.

"Sixteen."

The machine gun went dry. "Shove another belt in this sumbitch and get down the hill with the rest of them," said Billingsley.

O'Hanlon fed another fifty round belt into the gun, closed the loading gate and stared straight ahead.

The major and his men waited at the bottom of the hill. They could hear Hueys beating the air in the distance. They also heard the yammering of Billingsley's gun.

"Come on, Troy, get out of there," came the whispered prayers from the lips of the men who had drunk Budweiser with him.

"Who's the new guy with him?" someone asked. No one answered. No one remembered the new kid's name.

Billingsley kept firing, knocking down the black shadows walking up the hill.

The PT-76 tanks came to within twenty meters. By that time there were barely enough infantry left to cover the tanks. Billingsley's weapon made one solid crackling roar as it fired. The red glare of its muzzle blast reflected off the hull of the tank as the turret turned. The first shell of the cannon roared into the earth behind Billingsley and O'Hanlon, showering them with clumps of dirt.

The two Americans coughed in the cloud of smoke. Gasping for breath, they sucked in air that was now thick with the damp smell of freshly turned earth. Billingsley and O'Hanlon kept firing, the bullets ricocheting harmlessly off the turret. The next cannon shell passed through the dead center of the red glare. There was a rattle of small-arms fire and then silence.

THE NEXT MORNING a young Vietnamese girl stood over Billingsley and O'Hanlon. She sank to her knees and stroked O'Hanlon's cold forehead. His lifeless eyes were still open, the pupils dilated and fixed. She studied the fear locked in his glazed blue eyes for a few moments, then pressed the lids closed. She reached for the oval canteen hung on her NVA webgear, unscrewed the lid and tenderly splashed a small quantity of water on his face. Bunching up the tail from her long flowing blouse, she washed the red dust from his forehead and chin.

"Thuy Thien." An officer wearing a blue and white helmet called her by name. *"Chuan bi di."* Get ready to go.

She nodded. Deftly, she unbuttoned O'Hanlon's fatigue shirt, broke one of his dog tags from its beaded chain and slipped it into her pocket. She stroked his forehead as if he was an infant who had been laid to rest in its crib, then kissed the young American lightly on the cheek. She stood, slung her AK-47 over her shoulder and started down the road to rejoin her comrades. From a few yards out she turned around and muttered, "O'Hanlon, you are numbah one GI."

1

**SOMEWHERE IN THE
JUNGLE NEAR SONG BE
REPUBLIC OF SOUTH
VIETNAM**

U.S. Army Master Sergeant Anthony B. Fetterman was
beginning to like the time he spent wandering through
the maze of Vietnamese jungle, and that sense of enjoy-
ment bothered him because it meant he might become
complacent. That wouldn't have been a problem in a
blanks and umpires, blue team versus red team war
game. But in a combat zone with AKs and 16s mixing it
up, a complacent career soldier could end up buried in
Arlington National Cemetery.

Nevertheless the rhythmic moving and swaying of the
Southeast Asian tropical rain forest relaxed Fetterman.
The jungle noises he was accustomed to reassured him:
sounds like a dead tree limb falling through the branches
and then thudding onto the jungle floor; the earsplit-
ting, territorial caws, screeching and wing flapping of
brightly plumed birds.

Sometimes he even thought he could hear the over-
size plants and trees growing taller as they stretched to-

ward the sunlight filtering down through the trees. In some ways the jungle's familiar voice was hypnotic and soothing: the trance induced was not at all unlike falling asleep in front of the TV set.

At night the incessant howling of the monkeys swinging in the branches and the scurrying of creatures padding on tiny feet gave him comfort. The jungle made him feel at home because it was the one thing in his life that was a constant. The big, bad jungle had become no more threatening to him than the piney woods of Camp Mackall, north of Fort Bragg.

The supposedly hostile flora and fauna of the tropical rain forest were to him no more dangerous than those of the Uwharrie National Forest. Man, the outsider, the bloodthirsty intruder was Mother Nature's guilty son. As far as Fetterman was concerned, the rice-eating North Vietnamese regulars and the Vietcong with AK-47s in their grimy paws were the real threat.

Almost as if resting in eternal repose, Fetterman lay hidden in his jungle, flat on his belly. Overhead the leafy shade protected the back of his neck from the blazing sun while he looked down the crooked little trail with a model M-3A1 grease gun cradled in his arms. Under his belly, the mat of fallen, decaying leaves felt solid, warm and good.

Sergeant Fetterman was a small olive-skinned man with black hair and dark, cold hard eyes. He sometimes claimed that his lineage went back to the ancient Aztecs. Yet he didn't look anything like a combat soldier. Instead he looked as if he should be selling pots and pans door-to-door. Fetterman was someone you wouldn't notice if you walked past him on the street. That is, unless you got a good look at his eyes. There was a hardness in them that suggested Fetterman was a man who meant what he said and would back it up. He was friendly enough once you got to know him, but reserved until he decided whether or not you would do to go on patrol with. And the only way he would pass such a judgment was to take you out in the woods and see how you performed. And now he and two strikers lay hidden just off a trail in South Vietnam where NVA liked to roam.

Fetterman glanced over to a clump of overgrown foliage where he knew Krung was hidden. All Fetterman could see was a bush and a gentle breeze occasionally rustling its leaves. Krung, too, lay as motionless as a corpse on a bed of fallen leaves. Krung the Nung was an extraordinarily self-disciplined man, mused Fetterman. He had grown to trust Krung, even if he did have an ax to grind with the VC. But then, anyone who had been in the war more than a month was likely to get emotionally involved. Anyone who had listened in on the interrogations of captured VC grinning while they told what it had been like to cut a GI's throat from ear to ear when his M-16 had jammed. Fetterman shook his head. He wondered if the VC were that stupid or if they were simply brazen.

Fetterman looked ten yards farther down the trail where Kai, a Rhade Montagnard, had taken cover behind a clump of nameless bushes, wrapping himself inside a blanket of fallen leaves. Fetterman had never worked with Kai before; this was to be his test under fire.

Earlier that morning on a routine reconnaissance patrol the three of them had spotted footprints that had left the imprint of a tire tread on the narrow trail. Such a track was a dead giveaway because anyone who had been in-country for longer than a month knew the VC handcrafted their sandals out of old Michelin car tires.

The second clue had been what at first appeared to be aimlessly scattered pro-American leaflets. But a cynical Fetterman figured the fliers to be trail markers. What the hell, even the Vietnamese could have an ironic sense of humor, he figured.

And now, the three men waited in ambush to test both the enemy and Kai. They had brought little besides weapons with them to the ambush site: ponchos, canteens, ammunitions, grenades, claymore mines and detonators, trip flares and starclusters.

Fetterman's fingers traveled over the grease gun one more time. The bolt was cranked back and its ejection port covered. The weapon was ready to fire at the touch of the trigger. He was used to this crude but reliable .45-caliber submachine gun.

During World War II he had waded ashore at Normandy in water up to his armpits, an M-3 held high above his head. In the days of fighting that followed, and in spite of the fact that the weapon had been dropped in the sand and immersed in saltwater, it had never jammed. World War II, recalled Fetterman. It was the war that broke his cherry. The first man he had ever killed was a German soldier. In fact, it had been at Normandy that he quit counting the number of men he had killed in combat.

Some years later, during the Korean conflict, Fetterman had nearly frozen to death with an M-3 clutched in his icy grip. Even in the tropics he could remember what it had felt like to hold a hunk of cold metal in his hands, the warmth of his shivering body sucked out through his stiffened fingers. And later in the fifties, he had carried one of the submachine guns down the muddy jungle trails of Malaya while his Special Forces detachment advised the anti-Communist troops on the subtle art of counterinsurgency.

Even though weapons did not excite Fetterman in the seemingly sexual way they did some other men, he felt the grease gun to be almost part of him. And why not, he had argued more than once. He knew the weapon's capability, and its reliability had been proven to him time and again across the span of four wars. But to Fetterman's way of thinking, perhaps the most significant aspect of the M-3 was that it fired a bullet big enough to knock down a man, and you knew he wasn't going to climb to his feet and try one last time to stick a bayonet into your ribs.

And all of this form and function was derived from a weapon with humble beginnings. During World War II, the Ordnance Department had developed the M-3 in order to meet the need for a low-cost and easy-to-manufacture submachine gun. With its no-frills receiver stamped out of sheet metal, its low production cost rivaled the British sten gun, but the M-3 was more reliable. You could run over it with a deuce and a half and it would still kill Germans or Chinese, Malaysian Communists or North Vietnamese Communists. With a cyclic rate of 450 round per minutes, its recoil was easy to manage, while taking one of its thumb-sized slugs in the chest was not.

A sudden, hacking cough drew Fetterman's attention. A moment later a man stepped into view. About thirty meters down the trail walked a lone Vietcong with an AK-47. Slung across the VC's chest was a three-pocket OD canvas chest bandolier filled with extra magazines. Fetterman smiled as he noticed the telltale sandals with the tire-tread soles, and the ubiquitous black, baggy pants, their thin fabric the equivalent of jungle wash-and-wear.

Fetterman debated whether it was the right moment to spring the ambush. The enemy soldier could be alone, or he could be the point man for an entire company. Fetterman considered his options. If they let the VC pass them by, and nobody followed, he would have blown a chance to kill the solitary man. But on the other hand, if they let him walk by unmolested and a company followed in his footsteps, then the three of them would be so heavily outnumbered that it would be suicide to attempt an ambush. They would have to let the larger unit pass by as well and hope no one spotted them in their hiding places.

Without warning the VC stopped in his tracks. His eyes widened as he frantically brought the stock of his rifle up to his shoulder, aiming it in the general direction of the clump of bushes where Krung was hidden. Fetterman cursed silently, figuring Krung had been seen or heard. But Fetterman never got the chance to make the decision. His ruminations were interrupted by the crack of a single gunshot.

The impact of the bullet flipped off the VC's coolie hat and knocked him back a couple of steps. With the surprised look on his face that men have when they first discover they're wounded, he clutched his chest, fell to the ground and lay still.

Krung and Kai raced out of the bushes and ran up to the dead man, who lay flat on his back staring up at the sky with brown, lifeless eyes. Even in death the dead man's eyes were like mirrors into his soul. They had the look of betrayed trust and wonderment.

"Sergeant Tony. I kill him one shot," said Krung, proudly thumping his chest. A ray of sunlight reflected off his wrinkled, mahogany-skinned forehead. His jungle fatigues had been tailored to fit overfed American boys; on his frame the uniform hung as if he were malnourished, when in fact he was just skinny. The wiry Krung was Vietnamese Chinese, a Nung. When the Communists displaced his tribe from its land in North Vietnam his people had moved to the south to escape the bloodshed.

Standing next to him, Kai opened his mouth and reverently spit a gold Buddha into his hand and then let it dangle from a leather thong onto his chest. As part of his religious beliefs, the Montagnard wore the pendant looped around his neck. During times of danger, he popped it into his mouth so Buddha could protect him from death. It had worked so far. But at the moment, Kai disagreed with Krung's assessment as to who had killed the enemy soldier. He shook his head, vigorously. "No, I shoot him. I kill VC sumbitch. You miss very big."

Fetterman walked out of his hiding place and up to the dead man. He noticed that a single bullet had punctured the dead Cong's chest. There was some blood trickling down the side of the shirt, but not a lot. The bullet was probably lodged in his heart, Fetterman figured. He would have been dead before he hit the ground.

Unable to disguise his anger with Kai, Krung kicked the dead man hard in the ribs. Fetterman thought he heard the ribs crack with the impact. "My bullet kill him. You miss. Not me."

Kai responded in an excited voice, talking very fast. "*Dinky dau,* you crazy. You not hit him from where you stand now. Besides, you would shoot in the crotch. Only place you shoot is crotch. I hear stories about Krung. Only like to kill Cong in dick."

From what he knew of the situation it seemed obvious to Fetterman that both men had fired simultaneously. Neither man would lie about a kill. They both thought they were right.

Krung unsheathed his razor-sharp knife and held it menacingly in his grip. His eyes blazed in anger.

Fetterman wondered whether the Nung tribesman was intent on mutilating the dead VC or Kai. Fetterman dismissed the concern. After all, Krung's vendetta was against the Communists, and even if he was angry with Kai, it was unlikely that he would lose control and do something regrettable. But Krung's vengeance on the VC was a different story. His father had been headman in the village. A VC terror unit had rounded up and barbarously murdered every member of his family, except for his youngest sister. A dozen of the VC gang-raped and sodomized her, leaving her as a living reminder to the others in the village of what would happen to them if they supported the Saigon government. Not long after her night of horror, Krung's twelve-year-old sister put a bullet in her brain.

If any man had a reason to hate the Vietcong, it was Krung. He swore a blood oath on the souls of his ancestors, vowing to kill fifty of the enemy for every dead family member. It wasn't enough for him to simply kill the Commies. Krung emasculated the dead males with his knife, and had nailed all of the grisly trophies on a four-by-four sheet of plywood. Fetterman shuddered as he thought of the rotting flesh that emanated from the dozens of withered foreskins. Fetterman never asked Krung what he did to dead *co*, the dead female Commies. He didn't want to know.

Fetterman hooked his boot under the dead man's back and flipped him over onto his face. The bloody exit wound in his back was big enough to pass a fist through. He could see the spine and one of the lungs inside the cavity.

Both Kai and Krung got so excited in their anger that they lost their command of English. Each man was now babbling excitedly in his own native tongue, the words totally unintelligible to the other man.

Krung waved his razor-sharp knife in the air, sunlight glinting off the blade as he screamed about the accuracy of his shooting and insulted Kai's prowess with an M-16.

Fetterman, the diplomat, interrupted them. "You're both wrong," he said.

Mouths agape, Krung and Kai looked at the American.

"What you mean, Sergeant Tony?" said Krung, quizzically.

Fetterman rested the M-3 against the dead man's back, touching the muzzle to the exit wound. "Look at the size of that hole. That tell you anything significant about our little problem here?"

Neither of the Vietnamese said a word.

"It's easy as pie. You both hit him. Both your bullets went in the same hole in the front and came out the same hole in the back." Using the M-3 muzzle as a pointer, he traced a circle around the bloodied circumference. "Two bullets did that damage. Two bullets. Not one."

Standing in the steamy shadows of the jungle, all three men knew that only a single bullet had penetrated the Communist's body. But it was an easy way out of the argument, a way for both men to save face. And none of the good guys had to die.

There was an awkward moment of silence and then Krung nodded in assent. He spoke in a more normal

tone of voice. "You right, Sergeant Tony. Of course you
are. We both kill this man."

Kai said quietly, "You good shot too, Krung. You cut
his dick off if you want, Krung. Nail on your board with
others. Avenge your family."

"No, not this time." Krung slid his knife back into
its brown leather sheath and made a pouting expression. "Besides, him probably be too little to get good
grip on."

THE NVA UNIT WAS on the ground and moving rapidly
into the clearing. After thirty days of weapons and tactical training, they had walked the length of the Ho Chi
Minh Trail along the border of Laos and Cambodia and
into South Vietnam. It had taken them a little more than
two and a half months to move into position. Each of the
soldiers wore the same combat garb and carried the same
equipment.

They were dressed in a khaki-green uniform with a red
patch and a star on the collar, and on their heads wore a
tropical sun helmet made out of pressed fiber and bear-
ing a red star. Back home the NVA regulars were affectionately known as *boi doi*, slang for their hard hats.
Their armament consisted of three wooden-handled
grenades latched to their webgear and 150 rounds of
AK-47 ammunition in a waterproof plastic bag. Some
of the ammunition was loaded into the thirty-round
magazines that were stuffed into the three-pocket chest
bandoliers slung across their chests. They carried their
food in a canvas tube that held several pounds of sweet,
dried rice.

One of the NVA troops, Thuy Thien, skirted a series
of craters that dotted the clearing. "Are these holes in
the earth from bombs or artillery shells?" she asked

meekly. Thuy Thien was very careful to think out her questions before she voiced them to the cadre.

Her commanding officer was walking beside her. The fifty-year-old man stood five feet tall, his frail body topped with an officer's blue and white helmet that made him look a little taller. Sometimes Thuy Thien had seen him wear the campaign medal he had won for combat at Dien Bien Phu. He smiled as he answered the girl. "It's plain to see these are from a B-52 bombing run and not from the American artillery," he said with an air of authority. "You will notice the craters are clustered along a straight line rather than splayed in a wide and random pattern."

Thuy Thien's unit was returning to a battlefield they had withdrawn from only the day before. Her commanding officer knew the reputation of the cowardly ARVN soldiers, who as a matter of course could be counted on to drop their rifles in retreat and clutter a battlefield with abandoned ammunition and other equipment. Earlier that morning his scouts had reported beaucoup C-rations and M-16 ammunition left behind when the ARVNs had pulled out. Now, in the middle of the battlefield, they were about to harvest the booty. Very likely they would pick up enough equipment to supply a platoon and feed them for a week. The officer stopped next to one of the craters, shielded his eyes from the sun and looked up into the sky. He thought he could hear a helicopter off in the distance, and from the sound, figured it to be about ten kilometers away. That placed it far enough away not to be of major concern to his unit.

MOST DAYS Colonel Mick Angell rode to work in a helicopter, flying with a hunter-killer team: a deadly com-

bination of an OH6A Cayuse and AH-1G Huey Cobra
helicopters. The Cobras hovered at five thousand feet
while the loach darted along the ground, flying in wide,
slow, zigzags, searching for the enemy. The gunships
flew in a low-altitude circle that allowed them to cover
each other's backs and the scout helicopter.

In flight the loach looked like a pregnant mosquito as
it ducked below tree limbs, turned and twisted, flew so
low that it flattened the grass with its rotor wash, en-
abling the observers on board to spot hiding enemy soldiers.

A voice crackled in Angell's earphone. "Contact."
The scouting loach pilot had spotted enemy soldiers on
the edge of the battlefield. The colonel's sunburned face
broke into a wide grin; his hunch had paid off. Give
Charlie a piece of cake and then clobber him with it.
"Kill them where they stand," he ordered over the radio. The probe had caught an NVA unit in a very em-
barrassing situation.

The helicopters poured on the fire as Thuy Thien and
the others ran for the concealment of the palm grove.
Heart pounding, she dived flat behind a small rise in the
ground, right in the middle of six other young soldiers.
A series of explosions split the air behind her and she
joined in with the others as they shot their AK-47s wildly
into the air.

The Cayuse circled overhead and got out of the way.
In came the lean, wicked-looking Cobra gunship with
its miniguns blazing, ripping at the enemy soldiers
trying to hide. The Cobra made several more runs from
above and then the Cayuse came in at treetop level, its
miniguns rasping like a party noisemaker twirled rapidly. The leaves and grass whipped and jerked as if hit
by a violent windstorm. Moments later the ground shook

as the Cobra made another run with its air artillery rockets. The gunships took turns circling the area to keep the encircled NVA from escaping.

Rockets exploded on either side of Thuy Thien, the horrendously loud crump-crump making her eardrums ache. Then her eyes were filled with a bright white light. With a devastating sound, the explosion of a rocket picked her up and hurled her to the ground. She touched her fingers to the blood trickling out of her nose and realized that she had been deafened by the explosions. As real time seemed to slow down, she saw an orange blossom of light pick up a man ten meters away and throw him through the air over her head. As the shock wave washed over her a mist of warm blood sprayed against her face.

There were some last scattered shots, and then the noise that had reached a violent crescendo was followed by an eerie silence.

Thuy Thien stumbled to her feet and worked her jaw to make the ringing in her ears go away. The stench of fumes from the explosions clogged her nostrils. In a daze she saw her commanding officer lying on the ground. A rocket burst had torn him apart. One of his legs lay against a tree. Next to his bloodied torso lay his blue and white pith helmet, adorned with a piece of scalp. Other bits and pieces of his bloodied flesh were scattered around in the dirt. Thuy Thien started to scream but couldn't hear her own voice.

THE DEADLY SURPRISE had caught the NVA unit off guard and that pleased the colonel. His slicks, the troop-carrying Hueys, landed six squads, who followed the blood trails that indicated some wounded had managed to escape the withering fire of the gunships. Standard operating procedure dictated that they follow the trails until they found either a dead soldier or the blood vanished into thin air. A black buck sergeant from Chicago captured a hysterical female enemy soldier in a ravine and gunned down two others as they fled.

Excited with the outcome of the operation, the colonel ordered his pilot to put down so he could personally study the situation. As his helicopter approached the ground, still about forty feet in the air, the pilot flared, slowing their forward momentum. As the skids touched the ground, Colonel Angell leaped from the cargo compartment. The first bullet-riddled body he approached was lying facedown. The bullets had ripped into the torso, tearing out the backbone, leaving the pink, coiled guts stuck to it. That made the corpse a young kid, he noted. An old man's guts would be gray. Angell stooped to pick up the weapon and check the body for identification papers and other intelligence data.

Suddenly there was an abrupt staccato burst of automatic rifle fire from the tree line. Angell hesitated for a moment before throwing himself to the ground. In that split second of indecision a single rifle round pierced his side just below the armpit. The colonel grunted and went down. Like angry hornets the Cobra and the Cayuse took turns raking the trees where the shots had come from.

The colonel coughed up blood. The warm, red liquid oozed from the black-tinged hole in his chest. Teeth gritted, he covered the gushing wound and watched as pink froth bubbled between his fingers. He knew he was going to die before they could get him into surgery. As he was lifted into the Medevac helicopter, the Colonel hooked his bloodied thumb in the traditional okay and smiled at his men. "Give Charlie a piece of cake." He smiled. "Then clobber him."

2

**SPECIAL FORCES CAMP
B-34 REPUBLIC OF
SOUTH VIETNAM**

It was one of those days when he couldn't seem to get off the lima lima. Perhaps that would have been a more acceptable situation in the World back on Smoke Bomb Hill at Fort Bragg with the Seventh Special Forces Group or even with Tenth Group at Bad Tolz, Germany. But to U.S. Army Special Forces Captain MacKenzie K. Gerber, it seemed ironic and unnecessary to be tied up on the phone while smack in the heart of hostile Indian country.

Silently he cursed the Army's First Signal Brigade, its maze of land lines and microwave towers and the efficiency of the system that allowed people he didn't want to find him to take up his time. Silently he cursed the telecommunications systems that allowed mere phone calls to fuck up his day.

At that moment one very hot and miserable Captain Gerber sat with his elbows on the gray metal, government-issue desk, resting his chin on his hands. What seemed like gallons of sweat blackened his jungle fatigues across the back and armpits. In his office that did double duty as living quarters was a metal cot with a paper-thin mattress, and next to the cot stood a metal .50-caliber ammo can that he used as a nightstand. On it rested a Coleman double-mantle lantern painted Army olive drab. In front of the desk were two lawn chairs that Gerber had bought at the PX in Saigon. On one corner of the desk sat a half-finished bottle of soda: Gerber considered himself on duty and wanted to keep a clear head.

The construction of Gerber's hootch was a carbon copy of the thousands of other bunkers strewn across South Vietnam, consisting primarily of sandbag walls, reinforced roof, more sandbags and fast-growing mold that sprouted like a green blight on boots and jungle fatigues. And for variety the entrance was built in a zigzag pattern so that a near miss by an enemy rocket or mortar round wouldn't splatter shrapnel through the doorway and into the arms, legs and heads of the soldiers huddled inside for protection.

One benefit that Gerber appreciated about the bunkers was the thick walls, which were set into the earth and reduced to a dull roar the whining of the gensets that cranked out the camp's electricity. He liked that relative quiet provided by the wall's insulation. Outside the bunker and in the mainstream of camp life, the constant hum of the generator and the rattling of the diesel engine could nearly drive a man crazy, or at least give him a headache, if he dwelt on the noise long enough. And in the middle of a war there were more important things to drive a man crazy than kilowatt-hours in the making.

Gerber was a career officer on the list for promotion to major. A combat veteran of Korea and two tours of duty in Vietnam, it was just a matter of time until the tall, well-muscled man with brown hair and blue eyes made field grade. Then the responsibilities of command, and the hours of having a telephone cranked against the side of his head until his eardrums ached, would certainly grow even longer.

The first call of the day, the one that jarred him awake at 4:00 a.m., had been the worst. It had to do with his junior commo man, Sergeant Phil Gonzalez, who had been killed some weeks back. Phil had been a smiling, black-haired third-generation Hispanic with a wife and two kids in California, who had been in-country for barely a month. The last word he had from home was that his wife was pregnant again. There was no denying Gonzalez's death was a tragic waste.

Leading a reconnaissance patrol, Gerber had turned in time to see the frozen look on Gonzalez's face when the thing had hurled itself out of the chest-high elephant grass. The thing was a bamboo spear with a flame-hardened point lashed to a sapling that some VC had bent double like a bow. Unknowingly, Gonzalez had tripped its trigger, and the bamboo spear whooshed out of the grass and buried itself in his chest. The Medevac hadn't arrived in time to assuage the look of horror in the dying man's eyes.

Gerber had packed the belongings, written a letter and closed out Gonzalez's life. Or so it had seemed. But sending him home in a body bag hadn't been the end of it.

Weeks later, with Gonzalez dead and buried, Gerber had been unofficially dragged into a hopeless tangle with his soldier's group life insurance policy. The Army wanted to award the $10,000 to his adoptive parents, Roberto and Silvia. But his birth mother, a Hollywood and Vine streetwalker who had abandoned him as a two-day-old infant, was calling Gerber in Vietnam. She deserved the SGLI money, she demanded, in a loud and screechy voice. "Tell it to your congressman," he had patiently suggested. He had suggested several other things she could do as well, but that advice had been wisely offered under his breath. Diplomacy. The better part of valor, he had surmised.

Phil's adoptive parents didn't want any part of the money. They just wanted his Green Beret and sterling silver jump wings.

The TA-312 field phone rang, breaking Gerber's reverie. Incredulous, he stared at it. Impertinently, it rang a second time. He picked up the receiver and hoped it wasn't the whore, because if it was he already knew what he was going to say.

"This is Gerber and this is not a secure line," he said without emotion.

It was Bocker, calling from the commo room barely twenty yards away. Sometimes when his team sergeant called from such a short distance away, Gerber wondered why Bocker didn't just walk the few steps over to his hootch and talk to him in person. Bocker spoke in an excited voice. "We got Dirty Shirt borrowed from the First in Okie. He's already in-country. Nha Trang says they're through processing his paperwork and they'll chopper him in tomorrow morning, first thing."

"Outstanding," said Gerber, with a big grin. The day was looking better already. He was pleased and relieved to have another good man assigned to his detachment. He considered a good man one who was a known commodity, an NCO who wouldn't drop any unwelcome surprises on you in the middle of a firefight. "Shows you the power of a DA form 2496 and the chain of command," said Gerber.

"Yeah," said Bocker quizzically. "And what about Miss Alexander? Did Dirty Shirt really call her office at the Pentagon to get the ball rolling on this deal?"

"No. He took thirty days' leave in his hometown back in Ohio. While he was there he caught a military hop out of Wright-Patterson Air Force Base and flew down to Andrews in order to twist her arm in person. I guess when you want a TDY assignment, the old gal is the one who can make it all come together."

"Roger that."

Gerber furrowed his brow and his voice took on a more serious tone. "With Shirt on board, this means we can get down to business. Coordinate us some air out of here to Tan Son Nhut. Get us a lift, say, three, maybe four days from now. The delay will give Dirty Shirt a chance to acclimatize, get to know the other team members before we leave again. Build team integrity and all that good shit." Team integrity, thought Gerber. That was one of the things that made Special Forces work. After living together in the jungle for weeks on end and relying on one another to stay alive, everyone got to know every little detail about everyone else's life: hometowns, names of brothers and sisters, first girlfriends, favorite whiskey, favorite lovemaking positions. And a few days away from payday, if one SFer had a dime, and everyone else was broke, everyone had a penny.

"I never met Dirty Shirt," said Bocker. "He really color-blind? They don't let you in the Army if you're color-blind, do they?"

Gerber laughed. "Who knows for sure? He says he's color-blind, and that's why Vietnamese look fluorescent orange to him, and why they make such good targets in the jungle. I don't know about color-blind but he does have jungle eyes. He can spot VC hiding in the bushes better than the Yards can.''

"Well, it'll be good to have him along on our next excursion into the unknown wonders of the rain forest where—" Bocker interrupted himself. "Wait one."

Gerber heard the radio squawking in the background on Bocker's end as someone's SSB and static-altered voice talked on the radio. Gerber drummed his fingers on the desktop. He wanted off the phone so that he could get on with his paperwork.

Bocker came back for a moment, "Fetterman is calling in. You want to wait for a status report?"

"Roger that." Patiently Gerber stood by while Bocker talked to the ambush patrol deployed in the jungle outside the camp. They had been out since before dawn and were doubtless tired and hungry by now.

After a couple of minutes' radio procedure conducted strictly by the book, Fetterman signed off and Bocker came back to the phone. "Fetterman is on his way in," he said flatly.

"Any contact?" There were only two possible answers to that question, and both could hold onerous connotations. Gerber was prepared for either eventuality.

"Roger that. Says he had a bad day—he only got one of them. One KIA. Theirs. Our noses are clean."

Gerber breathed a sigh of relief. He had known Fetterman a long time. It was bad enough when a guy new to SF got killed. With old friends it was positively unnerving. "What's Tony's ETA?"

Bocker snickered. "He said Krung's not taking any trophies so they'll be back in time for the evening movie, good Lord willing and the creek don't rise."

"Anything else I should know about?"

"Negative. Unless you want to know what's showing at the Bijou . . ."

"Probably a John Wayne movie again."

"You got it. Civil war flick, *The Horse Soldiers*."

Gerber sighed. "I've seen it. Out." Gerber laid down the receiver. Absentmindedly, he stomped his black leather boot against the dirt floor of his bunker. The red clay mixed with sand clung to the sole, and clogged the seam where the sole was stitched to the boot's last. Stomping one boot, then the other knocked most of the grit off. All the while he cleaned his boots he wondered where the next mission would take his team: Laos, Cambodia, North Vietnam, or even into the southern reaches of China? He put the thought out of his mind. It did no good to speculate. It was no good to try and figure out a logical procession of order in a totally illogical war. No matter. He would find out where they would be tasked to deploy soon enough. No, too soon, he corrected himself.

The phone rang. He sighed. It rang again. Calmly, he drew his Model 1911A1 .45 automatic pistol and took careful aim at oblong green canvas brick with the black handset sitting on top. With both eyes open, his right arm fully extended and the front sight lined up right where he wanted it, he squeezed the trigger. Click. The hammer fell on the empty chamber. "Fooled you, you Commie motherfucker," he muttered. The phone stopped ringing. "There. That's better."

STAFF SERGEANT Antonius Crawley, better known in Special Forces as Dirty Shirt, stood in the terminal building of Hotel Three looking out the corner window. As he watched the helicopters operating from the field, he noticed the half dozen big square concrete landing pads that paralleled a wide grass strip and a chain link fence. He figured that the VIPs would get to land on the concrete while the helicopters on their way in from the outlying camps with mere soldiers on board would be required to set down on the grass.

While he waited for his helicopter to arrive, Dirty Shirt bore the stifling heat with a soldier's resolve. He looked down at his green beret in his hand, the stark yellow flash sewn above the leather brow. The flash designated him as a member of the First Special Forces Group stationed in Okinawa. He made a mental note to get a Fifth Group flash, black with the Vietnamese flag superimposed on it. And then he'd slip a few piasters to one of the camp mama-sans to have it sewn on his beret for the duration of his temporary duty in Vietnam. As prestigious as it was to wear a beret, it was even more prestigious to wear a beret from Fifth Group.

Dirty Shirt was a five foot nine Roman Catholic career soldier who had joined SF in the early days, before it had become President Kennedy's pride and joy. Back in the days before the beret was legal headgear and they could get in trouble for wearing one, but did so anyhow. It had been tougher to get into Special Forces before the Vietnam war had decimated the ranks.

To even be considered for SF, a volunteer had to have at least one hitch in the Army completed and be at least twenty-five years old. Then you had to make it through jump school if you weren't already jump qualified, and finally make it through training phases one through three at Fort Bragg and elsewhere. But embroiled in a war of attrition, SF had begun to take first-termers who were as young as twenty years old and Shirt had noticed the quality of the SF trooper was beginning to slip almost imperceptibly.

Nonetheless, after a decade spent in team rooms, covert operations and tours of duty with every one of the Special Forces groups, scattered from Africa's dusty plains to the German border near Czechoslovakia, Dirty Shirt Crawley typically only felt at home while involved in a mission. Even if it was nothing more than a training mission. It still ranked higher than garrison duty.

Shirt was pleased to be in-country and away from garrison duty in Okinawa. It was a temporary assignment in a war zone, but it still qualified as a respite from the mundane world of polished brass belt buckles and collar insignia and the ubiquitous folly of crisp, overstarched uniforms. He found the peacetime army too boring, too petty, too predictable. Little things bugged him constantly. At the commissary, captains' wives would shamelessly barge ahead of sergeants' wives at the checkout lanes. At the on-base schools, army brats regularly pulled their fathers' rank on one another in the playground.

In simple terms, garrison life revolted Sergeant Crawley. The stink of the greasy mess halls at breakfast nauseated him, as did the throngs of giggly soldiers in the chow line talking about how the night before a drunken WAC had taken on ten guys in the middle of the parade field after dark.

Such goings-on made him indignant. When he had first joined the Army in the early 1950s, rank had been slow in coming for him and all of the other NCOs in the Army. He had gotten out for three or four years and enjoyed civilian life. And even though he made lots of money, he didn't like it on the outside. Shirt wanted to be part of a fighting force with the heady feel of adrenaline coursing through his veins.

He closed his eyes and shuddered. He refused to be some pathetic character from a soap opera. Instead he longed to feel the thrill of Huey rotors whopping in the air overhead. He ached to hear the crackle of small-arms fire and the sensation of the impact and explosion of a mortar round bouncing him on the ground. While drafted GIs fought to live, he lived to fight because being close to death made Dirty Shirt feel very much alive.

Outside the terminal building, a Huey came to a hover, briefly turned its nose toward the tower and then settled to the ground, the rotor still spinning and the engine running. The large white hornet painted on its nose identified its unit as the 116th Assault Helicopter Company. The neat string of holes stitched along the length of the tail boom identified it as a helicopter that had come very close to being shot down. Without waiting for the bored-looking clerk behind the thin plywood counter to call out his name, Shirt grabbed his rucksack and M-16 rifle and ran out the door toward the grass.

Sidestepping a plump major, Shirt hurried to the helicopter. With a practiced step, he got up onto the skid so he could look into the aircraft commander's window. "I'm going to the SF camp at Song Be. You're my ride, right?"

The pilot, a warrant officer in his early twenties, nodded. "Climb in. I think there's room to squeeze in with the supplies." His face was drawn as if he had been flying too many hours, and with all of the action going on with the Tet offensive recently, Shirt figured he had been kept very busy.

Shirt found an empty troop seat, and fastened his seat belt. They lifted off almost immediately, the nose of the chopper dropping suddenly as the pilot tried to increase his airspeed. Flashing across the grass, he leveled off and pulled back on the cyclic. Shirt grinned from ear to ear, enjoying the sensation of speed. With the wind rushing through the open cargo compartment doors Shirt felt content.

Dirty Shirt's Huey flew from Saigon to Song Be at an altitude of three thousand feet. He didn't need to lean forward into the cockpit and search out the pilot's altimeter in the instrument panel in order to know their height above ground. He was familiar with the height from the way the ground looked from overhead, having flown so many times, in both peacetime and war. He also knew that was the altitude pilots liked to fly. It was partly pragmatic. In those days that was the favored altitude above ground level because it was hard for small-arms fire to reach a Huey's engine, transmission and fuel cells with their flickering fingers of green tracer-bullet death.

Dirty Shirt heard the sound of the rotors change pitch and prepared himself for the landing. The sleek Bell UH-1D helicopter circled Song Be Special Forces Camp B-34 at three hundred feet. Hanging onto the door gunner's M-60 machine gun mount, he boldly leaned out the door to look at the star-shaped outpost ringed by five strands of razor-sharp concertina and barbed wire.

The star-shaped fort was a throwback to the Army's Indian fighting days. Corrugated tin roofs reflected the blazing, tropical sun. Some of the structures seemed buried to the eaves. From experience he knew there would also be sandbags inside the roof to stop shrapnel. The buildings were virtual bunkers.

A few yards away from the building's sandbag walls stood a chain link fence; its job was to intercept rockets so the high-explosive warheads couldn't burrow into the sides of the bunkers and wipe out the men inside. The fence was only a month old and he could see at least three flame-blackened tears in its jagged sides already. Yankee ingenuity, he mused.

Beyond the camp's concertina and claymores lay the nameless ramshackle village consisting of hootches, mud streets and free-range livestock. Plainly visible from the air were earthen jars as big as oil drums and used for storing rainwater, cooking and fermenting *nouc mam*. Nouc mam was Vietnamese for the fermented fish oil that was liberally applied to rice and other foods. And from the years Shirt had spent in the Orient he knew its Japanese, Thai and Vietnamese names. He had even come to like its salty flavor.

Shirt studied the layout of the village. He figured that if the VC attacked, the villagers would make a run for the camp and pick up arms in its defense. The thatch-roofed hovels and the chickens and pigs were presumably on their own.

On the road that cut through the center of the village, a white bearded man stolidly plodded along, leading a horse-drawn cart that looked as if it had been fabricated from scrap lumber and salvaged car tires. Where rice fields bordered the village, a plump-faced young woman in a flowing flowery print dress and three knee-high children strode along the paddy dikes. When they came to a monkey bridge, a single, narrow and slippery log that bridged the canal, the four of them ambled nimbly across it as if it were as wide as a four-lane highway.

To the west of the camp, a paved black and unfinished runway bled off into a red slash of dirt where a team of Army engineers were running a gigantic bulldozer, pushing back the jungle. On the east edge of the runway, a cloud of purple smoke slowly drifted horizontally across the helipad. Noting the direction of the wind from the drift of the plume of smoke, the experienced pilot descended the last three hundred feet so rapidly that Shirt's ears popped. A moment later, the skids settled on the ground.

A detail of a dozen indigenous personnel swarmed like honey bees along both sides of the helicopter, and began to unload the cargo: cases of Budweiser beer, hermetically sealed metal cans of .30- and .50-caliber ammo for the machine guns, 81 mm mortar rounds and cases of C-rations. Dirty Shirt knew the beer would be consumed quickly, as soldiers the world over did with alcoholic beverages. Moreover, because the local water supply tasted so thoroughly of chlorine that it could turn a strong man's stomach, the beer was also used for brushing teeth and as drinking water. The machine gun ammo and mortar rounds would kill NVA troopers and VC foolish enough to make a run at the perimeter wire. The C-rations would be endured as the cost of doing business, the price one paid for putting on the rucksack and leaving the Saigon commandos to the sidewalk cafés and fresh food. But sometimes an indig from the village would trade C-rations for chicken or pork. And sometimes the helicopters would bring in steaks. But mostly, the fare was nothing more exotic than rice and C-rations.

Dirty Shirt walked a few meters away from the Huey and paused to read the camp scoreboard. On the four-by-eight sheet of plywood someone had painted Welcome to Song Be, Fifth Special Forces Group, Airborne. The information beneath showed the current statistics, including the number of VC and NVA soldiers who had been killed, wounded, captured, or who had surrendered outright under the Chieu Hoi open arms policy. Shirt nodded enthusiastically as he took in the numbers; this was an active camp with an aggressive campaign to bring the war to Charlie. But that was no surprise, given the reputation of the camp commander, Captain Jonathan Bromhead.

While Shirt read the scoreboard Bocker was on his way to the helipad. On the Huey's final approach to Song Be, he had talked on the radio to the pilot. Once it was safely on the ground, he had walked from his commo bunker down to the helipad to meet Dirty Shirt. Hand extended and a single step away from shaking hands, he heard an ominous tunking sound in the distance.

Simultaneously Bocker and Dirty Shirt yelled, "Incoming!"

The men unloading the cargo dropped their loads, scattered in all directions with a great deal of banter and kicked up even more dust. Rotors still spinning, the slick maxed pitch and took off in a near vertical climb.

Bocker figured they had about fourteen seconds before the mortar rounds began to drop onto the compound somewhere. He motioned to Dirty Shirt. "Come on, bunker's this way." Both men took off running and dived inside the shelter.

Safely inside the dank-smelling structure, the two SF sergeants heard the *whoomps* as the mortar rounds detonated. The Communists were firing in salvos. Both men braced themselves for the shock wave as the sandbagged walls of the bunker shook, knocking shaving kits, dog-eared copies of *Penthouse* magazine, and empty Budweiser cans onto the dirt floor. Dust clouded the air. More mortar rounds came crashing down on the compound as the enemy gunners pounded the camp. They seemed to be in no hurry, slowly and deliberately laying in the rounds. The explosions lifted dusty geysers in sudden clustered bumping shocks.

Shirt yawned, then reached through the cloud of dust to the floor of the bunker where a copy of *Penthouse* lay on its back. Shirt grabbed it, opened it wide and leered at the centerfold. "No way to treat a lady," he said reverently, blowing the dust away from her best features.

The enemy fired ten salvos. Forty rounds total. It lasted about five minutes. Then all was silent. The dust began to clear. The Vietcong's harassing fire was over for the time being. And odds were good that no one had even been killed.

As the dust settled around him, Bocker reached out his hand to Dirty Shirt. "Welcome to Song Be. Welcome to Vietnam."

Dirty Shirt smiled. After he had carefully closed the magazine and laid it on a bunk, he took Bocker's hand. "I think I'm going to like it here."

3

**RADIO RESEARCH
FACILITY PHU BAI
SOUTH VIETNAM**

It was four o'clock in the morning at the ASA Field Station near Phu Bai, and Spec Four Tom Davis sat at his position in front of a pair of Collins R-390A shortwave receivers. He was listening to a North Vietnamese radio operator trying to send Morse code.

Davis found it more than ironic that the United States Army had sent him halfway around the world to listen to a radio that had been built in his hometown during World War II.

The Collins factory was located barely a half mile away from the street where he lived. In fact, he had ridden past it on his bike a thousand times while delivering copies of the Cedar Rapids *Gazette*. Such are the fortunes of war, he mused, while adjusting the earphones and whirling the frequency knob back and forth to hear better over the crackling static. Once he had the radio signal tuned as good as it was going to get, he poised his stubby fingers over the keys of his manual typewriter,

typed in the time of day followed by his operator identifying number and began to copy the code.

After flunking the fall semester of his junior year at the
University of Iowa, Davis had enlisted in the Army Security Agency. If he hadn't enlisted, he would have been
drafted and sent to the infantry. Davis had no illusions
about the glory of carrying a rifle and being shot by little men in conical hats while he waded through waist-
deep rice paddies with human and water buffalo excrement bobbing on the surface.

His messiah had been the smiling, potbellied recruiter with a chest full of campaign ribbons, who had
regaled him with tales about the Army Security Agency,
a hush-hush branch of military intelligence. The beaming recruiter promised Davis that in the agency, and as
a member of the intelligence community, he'd never
have to make morning formations, never have to stand
inspections and never have to wear uniforms. Instead he
would work in civilian clothes, wear a trench coat and
be assigned to United States embassies overseas. Simply stated, his work would include real spy stuff. "CIA
will probably offer you a job in Berlin when you get off
active duty," the recruiter had confided.

"But do I have to go overseas?" asked Davis.

The recruiter leaned back in his chair and nodded.
"Yeah, that's the best part." He blinked, yawned and
wiped his mouth with his hand saying, "Probably get
assigned to Germany. I envy you, kid. I really do. Sign
here."

Throughout the eight weeks of basic training at Fort
Lost-in-the-woods, Missouri, the drill instructors left
Davis pretty much alone. They knew he had orders for
the ASA, and they didn't really know what that meant,
figuring it was better just to leave Private Davis alone.

They had their own careers to think about, their own skeletons in their own closets and they didn't want a revenge-bent recruit prodding into their affairs after he was snug as a bug in the ASA. After all, there were retirement benefits to consider.

About the time the network news went wild babbling about how they had caught a group of DIs and their compliant wives selling sex to basic trainees on paydays, Davis went on to learn Morse code at Fort Devens, Massachusetts, a country club fort with golf course, and Mirror Lake. And because of the buildup of the Vietnam War, company strength in the ASA training regiment swelled from the normal two hundred bodies to nearly one thousand. They lived in barracks that had been built during the First World War to house the doughboys and were subsequently condemned after the Second World War. They still stood in 1967, and were home for Davis the entire time he attended the ASA's high-speed Morse Code Intercept Operator School.

Each morning Davis and the other ASA students stood formation in uniform in front of the wooden barracks, whether it rained, sleeted or snowed. The abundant numbers of student soldiers overflowed the company streets. And every Monday through Friday, from 9:00 a.m. until 5:00 p.m., they crowded into oppressively hot classrooms to spend eight hours a day listening to di-dah-dit, di-dah-dit, and to screech at the top of their lungs, "Di-dah is Alpha. Di-dah is Alpha."

About once a week, someone in the classroom would leap up from his chair, yank off his earphones, grab his typewriter and run full-bore over to the plate-glass window and hurl it to its death. Calmly, two NCOs would walk over, take the brain-numbed man by the arm and lead him out the door. The next day the typewriter hurler would be back in his chair, equipped with a new typewriter, copying groups of Morse code with a wild look in his eye.

Davis himself never broke under the strain. He simply closed his eyes, mindlessly copied Morse code groups and dreamed about being assigned to Germany, where he planned on drinking copious amounts of dark beer and belly-whomping blond fräuleins on the pine needle floor of the Black Forest. It would be better than college. And when he got out he could continue school on the GI bill, all expenses paid.

Six months after he graduated from the Morse Intercept Operator school at Fort Devens, a bewildered and angry Davis found himself in a war zone, wearing starched fatigues and spit-shined boots and copying NVA army CW—continuous wave—Morse code transmission.

Two weeks before, when Tet had been at its hottest, the radio research compound where Davis worked had very nearly been overrun. That was not nearly as unsettling as the rumor that followed: that the MPs who stood guard outside their vault with loaded .45s had orders to shoot the ASA guys if they appeared to be in danger of being overrun and captured by the enemy.

As Davis intercepted the enemy radio traffic, he typed out the cipher text, five letters per group, ten groups of letters per line. Encrypted as it was, the gibberish made no sense to him or any of the other intercept operators who might glance at it. But the crypto wizards huddled in the back room, who lived and breathed code breaking, were pretty good at cracking the NVA ciphers. They were so good they could even break an encrypted message and tell him when he had flubbed a character, thinking it had been an *H* instead of an *S*.

Davis had been intercepting this particular NVA operator for the past eight months of his tour. The squiggly lines displayed on the oscilloscope verified time after time that it was the same man pounding the code key, using the same transmitter set week after week.

The ignorant slope hadn't even bothered to change vacuum tubes to try and throw off the electronic intelligence gatherers. If he had, his transmitter's radio fingerprint would have shown up in a different pattern and might have at least temporarily befuddled the American radio research endeavors. All the enemy operator had done in an attempt to evade interception was to change frequencies a couple of times. But whenever the transmissions disappeared from the usual freq, Davis patiently swept through the most likely frequencies, listening for that old familiar plodding style of his NVA friend. As a result of the painstaking search and the unfailing oscilloscope, he always found his errant man within a couple of days.

In spite of all the months of sending traffic, the NVA radio operator hadn't improved much. His heavy-handed dots and dashes were as crowded together as ever, making it hard to distinguish between individual letters of the alphabet. Davis muttered, "The dink may be slow, but at least he's not precise."

The trick chief, a career E-6 in charge of the midnight shift, walked the row of intercept operators seated in front of R-390 radio positions. He came to a stop behind Davis and leaned over the operator's shoulder to better see the enemy traffic as it was typed out on continuous-form paper. The E-6 grunted, "Same undecipherable stuff, huh?"

Davis flipped off one of the earphones, "Say what?" and continued copying code without missing a single character.

The trick chief raised his voice, as if he were talking to a deaf man. "We ran a DF on him. Cut, plotted and fixed his position at Phu Tho, Northwest of Hanoi up in the Red River Valley."

"That's interesting," said the Spec Four mindlessly. His thoughts were elsewhere, more specifically twelve thousand miles away and at the Mill, back in Iowa City. At his favorite college hangout a guy could get an eyeful of the braless hippie chicks with their melonlike boobs beneath tie-dyed T-shirts bobbing up and down in rhythm with their slow-paced steps. And simply by talking to a Mill waitress a man could tell whether or not she took a shine to him because if she did, her nipples would pucker, wrinkling the T-shirt's thin fabric.

Davis remembered Juicy Joyce, the folksinger, who regularly performed on the Mill's stage, singing her ballads about Joe Hill, the union man; Bill, the tough-as-nails lumberjack who stirred coffee with his thumb; or Dave, the hermit who lived in the cave and died in a blizzard. But most memorable were the butterfly wings embroidered across the seat of Joyce's bell-bottomed blue jeans. Davis began to feel the warmth of his erection pressing against the inside of his thigh. "Color. Brilliant bold, color. That's what I miss," he muttered aloud. "Rainbow red, blue and yellow. And round-eyed women with big tits. I'm sick and tired of olive drab, red dust and slant-eyed women and their singsong prattle. Sixty-seven days and a wake-up," he thought. "A little more than two months and I'm outta here."

Without a word, the trick chief rocked back on his heels, then moved down the line.

Davis sighed and deliberately stopped thinking about women. To do otherwise would have been senseless erotic torture. Satisfied that his man in the North was through beating his telegraph key for the day, Davis decided to dial up a little extracurricular intercept. He secretively tuned in the frequency of Radio Hanoi and listened to the English-speaking female commentator. Her name was Thu Huong, and she vehemently denounced the capitalist, industrialist nation, the United States of America. In a very eloquent manner she expressed her opinion of how its lackey puppet soldiers, the ARVNs, were sure to lose the war. "So go AWOL, GI. You imperialist Yankee soldiers." Such was the sage advice of the woman known as Autumn Fragrance.

While Davis listened to Hanoi Hannah, he thought about the newspaper article he had read about her. She had been educated at Cambridge; that explained her very proper English accent. She was pretty, and happily married. But the vile tone that her silky, smooth voice carried over the airwaves seemed to be in direct contradiction to the pristine image.

Hanoi Hannah continued her tirade. "To have peace our people must carry out the revolution. The Americans are cruel, savage and inhuman. In a village recently, American Green Berets from Song Be disemboweled a number of women, ripped out their livers to eat and laughed in satisfaction. They wrestled a number of little babies from their mothers' arms, cut off their heads and put them into plastic boxes, which they said would be sent home as souvenirs. Because of these and other atrocities the corrupt Green Beret imperialist army will be destroyed on all the battlefields...."

Imperialists, wondered Davis. He found himself wondering if he and other noncombatants were included in that category. Then he decided that it didn't matter either way, because he was going home soon. "Sixty-seven days and a wake-up," he muttered to himself.

GERBER HAD THE MEN assemble in the team house for what he jokingly called their last supper. The next morning a helicopter would arrive at Song Be to shuttle them to MACV headquarters where they would be assigned their next mission. With that in mind, they ate sandwiches, drank cold beer and passed a bottle of Jim Beam whiskey around the room. They avoided talking about the upcoming mission that had brought them together and instead concentrated on women and war stories. Fetterman was talking about dying in battle and how it was every soldier's eventual end. *"Memento mori,"* he said somberly. "Remember you must die."

Dirty Shirt threw out the question, "Anybody believe in the legends that the ghosts of warriors killed in battle are doomed to haunt the battlefields for eternity?"

Sitting next to him Kai nervously fingered the gold Buddha that hung on a leather thong looped around his neck, rubbing it like Aladdin's magic lamp. His religious beliefs held that the Buddha would protect him from death, and some Montagnards wore as many as two or three Buddhas for extra protection. But Kai could afford only one. As he worked his fingers, rubbing the gold until it felt warm, the brass bracelets that he wore on his right wrist click-clacked.

"I hear spirits when they talk me," said Kai. "Tell me to come hump boonies with them. Sometimes they talk.

Tell me not matter if I die. Life great circle. Soul come and go many times from stars to earth. Must learn lessons till get right."

Dirty Shirt stared off into space. "Life is a great circular movement," he said with great seriousness, his speech slurred by the whiskey and beer he had drunk. "The circle is the most perfect geometric pattern. It lacks nothing. Inside the circle complete balance reigns."

A smile cracked Kai's face as he let go of the Buddha and jabbed a finger good-naturedly at Dirty Shirt. "I like you, fella. You read wisdom Buddhist. You know philosophy real good. Real good."

Fetterman handed the whiskey bottle to Kai. "Ghosts talk to you, huh? I've heard the legends about the ghost armies that come out at night. The ones about the legions of soldiers killed in Vietnam. The Japanese, Chinese, French, Australians, Koreans and the Vietnamese themselves and how their souls stick around after they were killed. 'Cause they can't leave until somebody wins the war."

Krung interrupted him. "Not legends. Real. Up by ancestral home, every year anniversary Dien Bien Phu can hear dead French paratroopers cry out in pain, beg for morphine, ask for more ammunition, more water."

Krung looked to either side and started speaking in a muted tone, as if he didn't want the ghosts to hear what he had to say. "Sometimes I see VC with throat cut and wonder if French Foreign Legion not kill him."

Dirty Shirt's hackles rose as he imagined the feel of the icy fingers of death brushing up and down the length of his spine.

Krung brought the bottle of Jim Beam up to his lips, threw back his head and took a deep swallow of whiskey before he went on. "One time when my father lost on road at night, he see squad of soldiers, very bloody, helping each other walk. He thought Americans had invaded North, but soldiers speak French, told father been in horrible battle with General Giap. Soldier acting *dinky dau*, crazy. Say trying to find way home. Mens walk off in fog. Disappear. Father come into next town. Dien Bien Phu. People in town tell him that happen often, place on road he see soldiers longside graveyard for French soldiers killed at Dien Bien Phu."

"Ghost armies," said Fetterman, "the souls of soldiers wandering for all eternity." He chuckled lightly. "I remember when I was a kid, nineteen years old. A private pinned down on Normandy beachhead with dozens of dead men lying on either side of me. I swore I could hear the dead men laughing at me, making fun of me because I was afraid of death. I swear they dared me to join them so I could see there was nothing to be afraid of." Fetterman shrugged. "So in those quiet moments when I'm sorting out my life I wonder whether it was the overactive imagination of a kid, or was it the souls of the men." He shrugged. "Either way I don't suppose it matters. I was so afraid of the ghosts that I forgot to be afraid of the Germans."

Bocker snickered, "So what's the truth? Were you afraid of a ghost or were you afraid of the monsters that lurk in your own subconscious mind?"

Gerber said, "Now you guys know that Special Forces NCOs aren't allowed to be afraid of anything. It's not SOP. Straight legs can piss their pants in battle, but like it or not, we have a media image to maintain."

Kai furrowed his brow. "You not afraid? I sometimes afraid."

"No," said Fetterman. "Captain Gerber is joking. We're scared too. If we weren't afraid, that would be bad because it would mean we were crazy. The difference is we accept our fear. We know it's a normal human condition. The difference is we channel it, we use it to achieve our end instead of letting it cripple us. But like I said before, *Memento mori*. Remember you must die. If not in battle, may it be in bed beside a beautiful young woman."

All of the men raised their beers in a toast and said in unison, *"Memento mori."*

4

TAN SON NHUT AIRPORT
REPUBLIC OF SOUTH
VIETNAM

In flight somewhere northwest of Tan Son Nhut airport, Sergeant Bocker peered through the open cargo door of the Huey. Looking over the door gunner's shoulder and past the mounted M-60 machine gun with its barrel hanging down, he could see to the rear of their aircraft where the morning sun glinted off the Plexiglas canopy of a second Huey that trailed behind with Fetterman and Krung on board. After a couple of days' getting to know one another it was time to get on with the next mission. From their time in the air and the topography, Bocker figured their helicopter was about twenty minutes north of Tan Son Nhut.

Bocker fidgeted uncomfortably in the Spartan troop section. His back bothered him near the hips. He reasoned that the dull ache low in his spine was the price he paid for too many nights suspended in the low curve of jungle hammocks. The cost of doing business. And not surprisingly, during this latest tour of duty he often found himself fantasizing as to what it would be like to sleep eight hours uninterrupted on a real mattress with a pillow under his head.

He fantasized in intricate detail exactly what it would feel like to sit in a real chair, a plush, overstuffed recliner; to sit down and not have to expose his spine to the rough bark of a tree, or rely on another man's back for support. He wondered what it would be like to walk leisurely through the woods without an M-16 locked and loaded, without his ear cocked for any sudden sound, without his eyes alert for a bent branch or freshly fallen leaf out of place. He wondered what it would be like to walk down the streets of a country without so much filth and noise, without so many dead animals in the street.

Bocker was tired of the coppery odor of blood and the whiff of burst bowel commingled with the acrid smell of spent cartridges left on the battlefield. He shrugged, figuring that he was simply changing. But he wondered whether the insight portended good or bad.

Bocker searched the ground below him as if he were on a reconnaissance flight rather than a simple ride into Saigon. Talking was difficult because of the loud popping of the rotor blades and the roar of the turbine. All members of the flight crew wore acoustic helmets to better allow them to communicate among themselves. Without one, all Bocker and Gerber could do was sit back and look out the doors as the rice fields slipped away beneath them. Occasionally a village broke the monotony, the village usually no more than a few hootches with tin roofs that glinted in the sun, marking their location in palm groves.

Highway 1 from Go Dau Ha to Trang Bang flashed past. It was a two-lane paved road with light traffic consisting of Lambrettas, ox carts, Army trucks and jeeps. On either side of the thoroughfare the trees had been cut back fifty meters to prevent ambush. The only place where trees grew near the roadside was around tiny villages.

Bocker playfully nudged Gerber on the shoulder and pointed to the river below them coursing its way to the sea. "Do you see that?" the sergeant shouted over the engine noise.

Gerber nodded. "Oriental River," he answered rather matter-of-factly.

In appreciation of the event's simple beauty, the two comrades watched in silence as a sampan made its way upstream, its wake streaking the muddy, brown water white. And on both banks of the river the jungle foliage appeared so thoroughly green that it looked almost black. Bocker swallowed. In some ways Vietnam was one of the prettiest places on Earth. But for war, he mused. But for war.

From their bird's-eye view of civilization Bocker watched OD Army trucks moving on the roads in and out of Saigon, and farmers with coolie hats and their water buffalo working the rice fields around the outskirts of the city. Bocker was momentarily startled when the helicopter seemed to drop out from underneath him. Through the cargo compartment door he could see they were flying only three or four feet above the ground, racing toward a huge gap in the tree line about half a klick in front of them.

Helicopters were required to fly under the approach paths to Tan Son Nhut airport. Once through the trees they would pop up to five or six hundred feet to be cleared into Hotel Three, the helipad at the airfield.

Now at the western edge of Tan Son Nhut air base, they passed over the blackened hulk of a C-130 on the ground. The four-engine cargo plane was visibly dam-

aged by mortar rounds. The burned-out aircraft skele-
ton lay there inside its flame-blackened circle like a
lumbering elephant that had come home to die at the
ancient burial grounds.

Not unexpectedly the big American air base had been
a prime target early in the Tet offensive. Losing altitude
they overflew a bunker with sandbags toppled from its
walls, shell holes piercing the exposed bricks. Next to
the heap of rubble and smashed cement of the damaged
bunker was a great hole in the earth and a large quantity
of thrown-up dirt.

The crew chief noticed Gerber's stare. "Cong overran the bunker last night," he shouted at the top of his
voice. "Three battalions assaulted. Most of 'em are still
hanging in the wire. I hope we leave the bastards there
till they rot."

The helicopter turned left and now Bocker could see
the runways, the hangars and the sandbagged bunkers
of the Air Force complex at Tan Son Nhut. They gained
a little more altitude and then lost it all, coming to a
hovering stop a couple of feet off the ground. A second
later they touched down and before the pilot had a
chance to shut down the engines, Gerber and his men
had grabbed their M-16s and rucksacks and were running in a crouched position across the grass of the helipad.

A couple of hundred meters away from Hotel Three,
Gerber could see a shiny Korean War-vintage U.S. Air
Force F-86 fighter plane proudly displayed like a World
War II tank parked as a memorial in the middle of a town
square.

A dozen steps away from the helipad, Gerber and his
men walked past what looked like a bundle of old cloth-
ing. In reality it was a dead body on its back, contorted

by rigor mortis and bloated so badly by the heat of the sun that the swollen legs were about to burst the black pajama pant seams. The head was missing. And the white, powdery lime sprinkled over the sprawled body made the dead enemy sapper look as if he had been set on fire and then sprayed with a CO_2 fire extinguisher.

His flames had been put out, all right, thought Gerber. But from the string of bullet holes stitched across the dead man's chest, he figured the bore size of the extinguisher to have been about 5.56 caliber, and it hadn't been a gentle mist of carbon dioxide, but rather a lethal stream of copper-jacketed lead. "Say good-night, Charlie," muttered Gerber.

THEY ASSEMBLED at the terminal, an unpainted wooden structure under the tower. Master Sergeant Fetterman finessed a jeep from motor pool and they drove through Saigon to Pentagon East, the MACV Headquarters building, where they had an appointment with Jerry Maxwell, their CIA case officer. When they arrived at their destination, Sergeant Fetterman parked the jeep by a row of one-story buildings constructed with corrugated steel sides and roofs. The wooden frame windows were shaded by corrugated steel awnings that kept out the monsoon rains and blazing sunlight, depending on whether it was the wet season or the dry season. Fetterman looped a chain through the steering wheel and anchored it to the floorboards with a brass padlock. A thief could start the engine by flipping a toggle switch—there was no ignition key—but he would be unable to turn corners.

Walking abreast, the six of them passed by an admin area and an Army NCO who looked as if he had broken starch five minutes before. Gerber wondered how the sergeant kept his uniform looking so crisp in the humidity of Vietnam. The spit-and-polish NCO stared openmouthed at Gerber and his men's mud-caked boots and wrinkled jungle fatigues. Their eyes met as Gerber stared back, noticing the sergeant's name stenciled in black letters above his right shirt pocket: Cassidy. After a moment the square-jawed sergeant, who had gone to fat, looked away from Gerber and went back to the business at hand, delivering a blistering tirade to three young privates.

Dirty Shirt snickered to Bocker. "That guy's belly must've cost thousands of dollars in beer to grow."

The fat sergeant wore his highly polished helmet liner down low on his forehead, thereby shading his eyes from the sun all the while he screamed at the three young privates. "Keep yer goddamn dawg outta my company area. I'm getting tired of stepping in dog shit. Tired of policing up after yer mutt."

A tall lanky kid with scuffed boots and wrinkled fatigues, which looked as if they had been slept in ever since they were issued and signed for, pleaded his case. "With all due respect, Sergeant, we've had this conversation at least a hunnerd times. My young pup, Forsyth, is always on a leash, we never let him run free. It ain't our dawg doing the dirt."

Another one of the young privates calmly added, "Besides, our Forsyth is a little puppy. That dog crap you're complaining about is big enough to be from a human."

"Yeah," said the third private. "It's either somebody else's mascot or one of the zips that don't like you is just taking a dump to piss you off."

The sergeant stood with his hands on his hips. "I see," he said in a very quiet tone of voice. He nodded once, lifted the flap from his black leather holster, pulled out his .45-caliber automatic pistol and waved it carelessly in the air.

The three privates just stared openmouthed at the sergeant and his steel-gray automatic pistol.

"I see from the looks on your faces you got the deal figured out. You just keep the dog the fuck outta here. Or I'll shoot your puppy and give 'im to the zips or the Korean Roks to cook with their white rice." The sergeant holstered the pistol, turned and waddled off toward the cluster of white-painted administration buildings, as if he was the sheriff in a Western, who had just told a gang of outlaws to get out of town.

Bocker and Fetterman exchanged glances. Bocker spoke first. "Guys like him give humanity and career-soldiering a bad name."

Fetterman agreed. "I've seen it before. He's probably got a small dick and trying to compensate for the shortcoming by being a big asshole."

Dirty Shirt muttered. "Wonder if his IQ is as big as his boot size?"

"Like my aunt used to say," said Gerber, "what goes around comes around. I expect he'll step on his own teeny wienie one of these days."

"You're right," said Dirty Shirt, jabbing a finger menacingly at the fat sergeant's ass as he waddled away. "Guys like him always get what's coming to 'em. That is, if I have anything to do with it."

The American MPs at the gate of the compound didn't challenge Gerber and his men because the comings and goings of Green Berets accompanied by indigenous personnel were a familiar sight. The six men walked to the front of the MACV building. Gerber pushed open the first of the large glass doors, and led the way through another set of doors and on into the air-conditioned headquarters building where the air temperature was as cold as arctic ice.

The MACV HQ typified a problem that, try as he might, Gerber was never able to surmount. It aggravated him beyond comprehension that chairborne commandos were allowed the privilege of picking over new equipment and food seemingly the very moment the stevedores set it down on the docks at Cam Ranh Bay. The same weasels who appropriated the ships' cargo were also quartered in buildings with roofs over their heads while the men who really fought the war, bled their veins dry and then died in the mud, were relegated leftover food and equipment. Somehow it didn't seem right.

Gerber and his men shivered while they walked along the tiled hallway. "Wait a minute, what's this?" said Fetterman. "Here's some new stuff."

The men paused in front of one of the bulletin boards, where someone had tacked up a National Liberation Front propaganda leaflet aimed at subverting American soldiers. It read: American servicemen. Don't fire at and spray suffocating gas at our people's air and cannon shelters. Don't destroy our crops, kill domestic animals and plunder our people's property. Repression, terrorism, massacre, house burning, women raping... are not the democratic American's ideals. Stop spraying noxious chemicals in South Vietnam. Stop the war of aggression in South Vietnam! Bloods of American and Vietnamese youths have been shed too much! Peace in South Vietnam and repatriation of all U.S. troops. (signed) The South Vietnam National Front for Liberation.

"Okay," said Gerber. "It works for me."

Next to the propaganda appeal was a citation for U.S. Army Special Forces Master Sergeant Charles E. Hoskins, Jr., detailing how he had posthumously won the Congressional Medal of Honor. Fetterman read the citation aloud: "While Sergeant Hoskins was preparing a Vietcong prisoner for transport to the base camp, the enemy soldier grabbed a hand grenade from the sergeant's webgear, armed the grenade and ran toward American and Vietnamese soldiers standing a few feet away. Leaping on the Vietcong's back, Sergeant Hoskins forced the grenade against the enemy soldier's chest and wrestled him to the ground. He then covered him with his body until the grenade exploded. The blast instantly killed both men, but Sergeant Hoskins's action saved the other members of the command group from death or serious injury. Born in Ramsey, New Jersey, in 1924, Master Sergeant Hoskins had entered the Army in 1943."

Having been assigned to the same A-team with him back at Bragg, both Fetterman and Bocker had known Hoskins, his hometown, his Thai wife and three little kids. Bocker spoke first. "He had a basic load of balls, Chuck did." Fetterman nodded, then pointed down the hall to the other side of the cage. "Come on. Let's get this thing with Maxwell over with. I think I feel a drunk coming on."

In a more somber mood, the SFers descended a stairwell and at the bottom were stopped by a Spec 4, who stood in front of a gate of iron bars that ran from floor to ceiling. The pimply-faced guard asked for ID cards, then used a field phone on a small desk to verify that someone inside knew Gerber and would meet him.

Satisfied with the credential check, the MP logged them in, opened the cage, let them through and locked the gate behind them. Gerber turned down another corridor lined with cinder-block walls that were damp with condensation. Rust spots stained the tile floor where metal chairs, tables and file cabinets had once been situated but had later been removed. Gerber halted in front of a dark wooden door and knocked. "It's us, Maxwell."

The man who opened the door was short. He had dark hair and dark eyes and a sunburned complexion. He wore a white suit and a thin black tie that was pulled out and his collar was open. "How's tricks, guys."

Gerber went in first. "I'll warn you, Jerry, none of us are in a very good mood." The others followed him into the room in single file. Inside the office one wall was lined with a row of gray, four-drawer filing cabinets. The one in the corner was massive, with a combination lock on the second drawer.

A battleship-gray metal desk, its top heavy with papers and manila file folders was shoved into the far corner. Four empty Coke cans were lined up against the edge closest to the wall. A small chair sat near the desk and a larger one was placed next to it. Against the wall was a stack of folding chairs that Gerber figured had been brought just for the meeting that would commence after the exchange of pleasantries. A single picture depicting cavalrymen fighting Sioux and labeled *The Wagon Box Fight* hung tilted on the wall. Because the office was below ground and without windows, the fluorescent lighting gave it an eerie glow. It was the kind of place where you would never be able to tell what time it was without a clock. And even though the supercooled air from upstairs did not filter down to the lower level, it was still cooler in Maxwell's office than outside the building.

Maxwell smiled as he stood in front of his desk. His face was drawn and his black hair was damp and plastered against his sunburned forehead. With the dark circles under his eyes and stubble dotting his face, he looked utterly exhausted. The backs of his hands were covered with scratches. His rumpled white suit hung on his gaunt figure as if it were another man's clothes; it was obvious the CIA man had lost twenty or more pounds in the tropical heat.

Maxwell grabbed his pant legs by the knees and lifted them up to midcalf to show off a new pair of boots. They were similar to the standard-issue combat boots in that the lowers were black leather, but circling the ankles was OD green nylon. And the soles were cleated to provide better traction in the mud.

The SFers formed a semicircle in front of Maxwell to get a better look at the new boots. Maxwell stood there proudly displaying his ankles.

"What are they, German made?" asked Fetterman. "Leave it to the Krauts to design a good pair of boots."

Dirty Shirt sank to his haunches. "Nah. They got the look of U.S.A. on 'em."

Gerber folded his arms across his chest. He knew what kind of boots they were. "So that's what the new jungle boots look like. But that doesn't explain what you're doing with them, Maxwell. Black market? That's one more pair diverted from the guys in the boonies who really need them. Not that any one of us could use a pair. You spending much time in the field these days, Maxwell? Don't answer that. Don't. I know you'll lie through your teeth."

Maxwell waved away Gerber's admonition, beaming proudly. "Been wearing this pair for eight days. Almost broken in. I think they're just wonderful."

Fists clenched tightly to resist primal urges, Fetterman bit his lip and held his stomach muscles taut.

Dirty Shirt stared straight into Maxwell's eyes and said somberly, "During World War II when guys from the 101st Airborne caught a straight-leg infantryman with jump boots on they'd hold him down on the ground, cut off the uppers and leave the guy with a pair of Corcoran low quarters. They look real nice spit-shined."

"Guys. Come on," said Maxwell with a grin devoid of mirth.

"He's right," said Gerber. "Let it die. It's not worth it. This time."

Maxwell clapped his hands together and breathed a sigh of relief. "Yeah, we have business to discuss, then we can go downtown like we planned. You guys up for a night on the town?" Without waiting for an answer Maxwell spun to his desktop and picked up a manila file folder stamped on the top and bottom in bold red letters: Top Secret. Maxwell opened the folder and Gerber could see a sheaf of papers also stamped Top Secret. "I don't know why they even bother classifying some of this stuff." Voice cracking, he held the file protectively close to his chest. "You hear about the battle for Lang Vei yet?"

Gerber knew where Lang Vei was on the map. Detachment A-101 was located up in I Corp along the Laotian border and on Highway 9 just down the road from Khe Sanh. "No. I've been somewhat isolated out at Song Be getting ready for this mission. But as near as Lang Vei is to Khe Sanh and the way the VC have laid the siege on the Marines, it only makes sense they'd want to hit Captain Willoughby's team."

Maxwell spoke slowly, as if he were telling a mother that her only son had been killed by a drunken driver. "Lang Vei fell last week. They were overrun." His hand was shaking as Gerber took the file from him.

Gerber could feel the tension in the room. To a man the biggest terror of all was the fear of being overrun. It chipped away a little each day, threatening to drive a man over the edge. Gerber himself could not conceive of anything worse than the specter of being overrun by a human wave advancing to the sound of the NVA bugles. He had thought about it a lot, why the fear dug so deeply into a man, and had come up with a good answer. Not only was it the fear of dying a violent death, but also the fact that the enemy would resort to a human wave violating morality. There was no chance for a fair fight.

Gerber often wondered what went through the minds of the Seventh Cav at Little Big Horn and recalled how, near the end, some of the cavalrymen shot themselves rather than surrender to the Indians. And once you died in battle, whether on the American prairie or in Southeast Asia, the suffering wasn't over. Your soul would have to watch as the tribal American Indians or cocky NVA troopers pulled off your boots and methodically stripped your body of its uniform and wristwatch. And once the victorious enemy faded back into the hills or the jungle, the body might not be recovered until after the gnawing rats and bugs had done their work, ensuring a closed casket ceremony **with** an American flag draped across your remains.

Not much had changed in a hundred years, thought Gerber. The Army had not been effective against the Indians and was not doing much better with the VC.

"So tell us what happened at Lang Vei," said Gerber.

"Yeah, sure," said Maxwell. "They hit A-101 about a week ago, on the sixth. With amphibious tanks, PT-76s." The CIA operative had everyone's full attention now as the dumbfounded team drew closer together to hear the rest of the story.

In a somber voice Bocker said, "Jeez, tanks. How did they get tanks down the Ho Chi Minh Trail?"

Maxwell threw up his hand in the characteristic I-don't-know shrug. "God knows these are resourceful people. They have resolve. Nothing they do surprises me anymore. Absolutely nothing. Hell, if I was the Navy I'd be on the lookout for an NVA battleship chasing down the carriers."

Gerber read aloud from the report, telling the men in the room how the five NVA amphibious and a large number of NVA troopers had made a nighttime assault on Lang Vei.

Maxwell nodded. "Early on, Intel knew the tanks were in the area. In fact, an FAC spotted them on the road, called in an air strike and splashed one. The others hightailed it." He shrugged. "But everyone figured the surviving armor was going after the Marine combat base at Khe Sanh."

Fetterman slowly shook his head. "I've been through a siege more than once. Been overrun." He looked to Gerber.

Gerber nodded as he remembered the incidents Fetterman was referring to. "Plei Soi and Camp A-555." In both instances they had very nearly been overrun and wiped out.

Fetterman shuddered visibly. "It's bad enough to hear movement in the wire, pop an illuminating flare and find out it's a battalion or two of men. But tanks in the wire. No, thank you."

Gerber read aloud from the report, which told how many of the light antitank rockets, the LAWs, had misfired, and how the ones that weren't duds had had little effect on the seemingly impregnable armor.

Another complication had been the camp's contingency plan; the Marines at Khe Sanh were supposed to reinforce the outpost with two companies of riflemen. But when called on to do so, they didn't, fearing an ambush if the relief force were to come in on the highway. And because it was night and the enemy had armor they declined an airborne assault with helicopters.

Maxwell summed it all up. "So we lost the camp, and the enemy won its first engagement with armor. Out of twenty-four Americans at Lang Vei, ten were killed or are MIA, and eleven were wounded. Out of the five hundred indigenous personnel, two hundred are either dead or missing and another seventy-five were wounded. Nearly all of the camp's weapons and equipment was destroyed. And the bottom line is that right now, today, in this building, there's some very worried brass who wonder if Khe Sanh isn't next on the chessboard. They wonder if Khe Sanh is going to hold up under its siege."

Gerber closed the file folder. "So why is it we have been summoned into the wizard's lair? One need not be too bright to figure out our mission is at least in some way related to Lang Vei. What is it? We're being tasked with assassinating General Giap?"

Maxwell stroked his chin as if suddenly enamored of the idea. "Quite frankly, I hadn't thought of that, but it's not a bad idea. But of course we would never commit such a heinous act."

Gerber, Fetterman and Bocker said in unison, "Right."

"However, what I do have in mind for you will be just as satisfying. Challenging, certainly, but nonetheless this is one you can really sink your teeth into."

"What's that, Jerry? We're finally going into Laos in the open, no more covert, behind-the-lines missions?" said Gerber sarcastically.

Maxwell pursed his lips. "I can't tell you."

Fetterman questioned Maxwell's knowledge of his parentage, then said, "What is this happy horseshit? You're playing cutesy games with us now, we're supposed to guess in twenty tries or less. I know. Your work is so fucking spooky and secret, you don't even know what you're doing."

Gerber handed the Lang Vei file back to Maxwell. "Sergeant Fetterman has raised a valid point. If we don't know what mission we've been tasked with, how are we supposed to act on it? Tell me there's a reasonable answer to this bait-and-switch routine you've just handed us."

"Trust me," said Maxwell. "We're waiting for a courier flight to come in from Da Nang. The Air Force's intel's been delayed. A plane crashed rather inconveniently and the skinny on your, uh, target won't be here until tomorrow. You probably saw the 130 on the way in. Anyway, I won't take a chance and breathe a word about it to you or anybody else, until I have all the pieces of the puzzle in front of me. Even though this is a piddly little mission, why take a chance at compromising it and screwing up my career? Look, guys, by next year I'm going to have a nice quiet little office in Virginia. The last time I worked there, President Eisenhower had just laid the cornerstone for the building in Langley. I've been a good little boy and maybe they'll let me out of the back alleys for a while and I can fight commuter traffic and sleep in on Saturday mornings. In the meantime, why don't you guys shake the sand out of your boots and have a mini R and R right here in good old Saigon? You hungry? I said I was buying.''

AFTER THE CAB picked them up near MACV and let them out in downtown Saigon, the soldiers and the CIA man walked the streets in silence. There was plenty to see, Gerber noted. During long weeks in the jungle, his sense of smell always improved markedly, as did his vision.

A large black Citroën rumbled past, leaving a noxious blue cloud of smoke in its wake. Gerber sneezed and his nose started to run. Soon his eardrums ached from the clamor of the Citroëns and Honda motorcycles that clogged the tree-lined streets. He knew from experience that the sudden transplant from the boondocks to a metropolitan area was very nearly sensory overload for the first couple of days. He knew that little by little, each day he spent in civilization, his five senses would be dulled more and more until he returned to the jungle. Then they would become fine-tuned once more.

Fetterman was content to gaze unabashedly at the architecture of the graceful buildings. The study was a pleasant diversion from the simpler lines of the hootches and pigpens near Song Be and all of the other A and B camps. The government buildings were easy to recognize; with their French style of architecture the edifices could have been standing in Paris on either side of the wide boulevard the Champs Elysées. Fetterman had been there during the liberation in 1945.

The slums were unmistakable, too, but not for their resemblance to the City of Light. The shacks were pieced together out of cardboard and packing crates, refuse from U.S. Armed Forces war matériel. On one block they passed Indian curio shops bulging with useless brass trinkets, butcher shops with the sickly sweet smell of death wafting out to the street and grocery stores bulging with hundred-pound bags of white rice.

Without warning, a pleasant-faced six-year-old boy with a dirt-smudged face stepped out of the sea of humanity and approached Bocker. The wary sergeant recoiled instantly, fearing the shoeshine boy might be a VC agent armed with a live grenade or cocked pistol.

With a look of fascination in his sparkling eyes, the giggling little Vietnamese boy stepped directly in front of Bocker and then ran his diminutive fingers up and down the man's hairy forearm. Bocker figured the boy was harmless, so he dropped his guard.

Maxwell grinned and spoke directly to Bocker. "Some Orientals say the reasons Americans have hairy chests is because they are primitive, like the monkeys still swinging in the trees. And that's why we don't understand the nature of jungle warfare. Which is a contradiction in terms, of course. If we're monkeys, wouldn't we understand war in our own element better than they do?"

Bocker looked at his own hairy arm and then looked at Maxwell's open shirtfront and hairless chest.

"It's a form of fur, you know," said Maxwell, grinning. "Feral fur."

"That isn't particularly funny," said Bocker, trying to maintain his fading grin.

"I didn't mean it humorously."

The little boy held out his hand, palm upward toward Bocker. "You numbah one GI. Give me money. Okay?"

Bocker shook his head.

The boy's smile melted into an evil scowl as he stepped back.

Bocker absentmindedly scratched the back of his head. "Guess that must make me a number ten. A bad guy." He shrugged.

The street urchin shook his head and pointed an accusing finger at Bocker. "No. You *xau lam*. Numbah ten thousand. You horrible fucking Joe." The kid had put special emphasis on the word horrible.

Bocker's grin faded.

The boy crept back toward the street and the Americans continued walking. A couple of minutes later the incident was forgotten.

Fetterman had picked up a guide to the customs and culture of Vietnam and read from the book's pages as they walked down the street. "Hey, listen to this: 'Due to changing circumstances, it is advised that you check with your embassy before embarking on visits outside of the major cities.'"

"Does that mean us, you figure?" said Bocker, with a straight face. "Next time we send out a recon patrol, maybe we should land-line the embassy to find out whether we'll be safe in the jungle. You never know, we might get mugged or something."

Gerber gave them a tight-lipped grin. "Good thing you found that warning. We won't bother the embassy, though while we're in Saigon we might as well be on the lookout for pickpockets and con men. Really, you can't trust the VC secret agent any farther than you can throw him."

"Or her. Don't forget the *co*," added Fetterman.

"Or it," said Krung.

"Seems to me this book is advising us to be careful who our friends are," said Fetterman.

"Maybe they're talking about Maxwell," said Bocker. He threw a mock punch.

Maxwell ducked and they all laughed.

"Anybody hungry?" said Gerber, stopping on the corner.

"Yeah," said Maxwell. "You want to get something to eat. How about some *pho*." *Pho* was a soup sold on street corners, and qualified by Vietnamese standards as a meal any time of the day or night.

"Nah," said Dirty Shirt. "You never know what's in it."

Gerber shook his head. "No. I'd rather something more substantial."

"You guys like lobster? The My Canh Restaurant serves the best lobster in town," said Maxwell.

"Wait a minute, I thought My Canh was in Nha Trang next to François?" said Fetterman.

"You're right, there's one there, too. Hell, I don't know, maybe it's a chain. You want lobster or not? I'm still buying."

5

MY CANH RESTAURANT
SAIGON

An hour later they had finished eating dinner, and the conversation had predictably turned to the recent Tet offensive.

"Well, Maxwell, how's the war going?" asked Gerber good-naturedly. "Do Uncle Ho's legions have any last gasps of breath?"

Maxwell shrugged. "Who knows? Although I can tell you, all through the region we're seeing guerrillas as young as twelve and as old as seventy-five in the enemy ranks. And more and more NVA regulars are being sent south to serve as replacements in battered Vietcong units."

"Sending NVA troops is both good news and bad news."

"How do you figure?" said Maxwell.

"Well, obviously it's good news because it means the VC are suffering heavy losses. But it portends bad, too, because it means they're committed to sticking it out, and it means we're going to be going up against better trained and disciplined regulars."

"I agree," said Maxwell. "I agree. This is a war where all constants are variable."

"Bamboo technology or not, Tet doesn't look like it's being launched by an army on its last legs," added Fetterman, with a puzzled look.

Maxwell nodded. "Charlie got lucky a couple of times, that's all."

"I hear it was a lot like the Battle of the Bulge," said Fetterman. "Only instead of German troops being where the Allied command didn't think there were any, it was VC and NVA. And instead of machine-gunning POWs at Malmédy, the VC massacred three thousand civilians outside of Hue and buried them in a mass grave."

Maxwell nodded, then said wryly, "Like a cat busy burying his shit. Of course, the press isn't mentioning that little outrage. After all, if American troops didn't do it, it won't sell newspapers."

"They are mentioning that the NLF overran the U.S. embassy," said Bocker.

Maxwell thumped his chest. "I was pinned down at the embassy that night. The MPs took it on the chin. Two men were shot down when sappers blasted their way in. Two more were killed and five wounded in the six-hour battle to take back the grounds. The VC were armed with automatic rifles, rocket launchers and heavy machine guns." Maxwell clenched his fists and added angrily, "The brave ARVNs did nothing but lock their doors and hide. I didn't just say that by the way."

"I know," said Gerber. "I was there, too. Remember?"

"Right," said Maxwell. "There were so many things going—"

"We break General Giap's back?" interrupted Gerber flatly.

"ARVN intelligence estimates North Vietnam's army commander in chief suffered fifty thousand casualties. Thirty thousand of the little gooks were killed outright." Maxwell grinned. "They came to the south to die by the thousands. Even as we speak, General Vo Nguyen Giap is trying to replay Dien Bien Phu up at Khe Sanh. His 304th division was at Dien Bien Phu back in 1954, at Khe Sanh last year, and we're positive they're back again this year. No problem, his little bastards in black pajamas and pith helmets are coming out in the open and we're slaughtering 'em."

"That's not what the papers say." Gerber laughed. "To hear the press tell it, the lunar New Year attacks were a great psychological victory for the bad guys."

Maxwell threw his hands up in the air. "Well, if you read it somewhere, it must be true. Writers don't lie. What do I know?" He laughed and waved away his previous statement. "There are 627 reporters accredited in Saigon. That's an awful lot. Most of 'em are kids. Good writers but too short on time in the harness to understand all they know about what they're writing." Maxwell pressed his point. "The Communists do everything for psychological effect. And they do that because they understand the American press. They use the American press. There is no question about it."

"It's not like the old days," said Fetterman, shaking his head. "Back in the Second World War the war correspondents lived with the troops full-time. Lots of them died in the trenches and on the battlefield right alongside the other dogfaces. Good reporters like Ernie Pyle and John Bushemi."

Maxwell nodded. His voice sounded tired. "Other than our mutual acquaintance, Robin Morrow, and a couple of other exceptions, not one of the reporters has been out in the boonies on an overnighter. And that's a major complaint. No one, and I mean no one has seen them out there. Hell, all they do is hang around the Carasel Hotel and get drunk."

They were all silent for a few moments, sipping the last drops of coffee. Fetterman sat there with his fingers pyramided for a moment and then blurted out, "Am I getting paranoid, or on our way in this morning did I notice that most of the major installations, like the revetments for the fighter planes and the airstrip and builders, weren't even touched by the sappers? Why?"

Maxwell grinned, jabbing his finger in the air twice for effect. "Good. Good. Very observant. Between you and me, they did leave a lot of stuff alone. Hell, it wouldn't be in their best interests to do it any other way. They don't want to damage it and have to rebuild what's already in place. They want to save it, so it's intact when we leave and they take over. That's what they're counting on, these are very patient people."

"If we pull out like the pinko peace freaks want, the Commies will have the largest army in Southeast Asia."

"Bingo," said Maxwell.

Dirty Shirt nudged Bocker, then whispered to him in a derisive tone, "Bingo. Did he say Bingo?"

Bocker raised his eyebrows.

Maxwell didn't notice, he was on a roll. "The problem we're faced with, all due respect to our commander in chief, President Lyndon Johnson, is that that ill-advised son of a bitch listens to these Washington, D.C. belt-line think tank guys, who figure our strategy ought to include a two-salient thrust. One salient being military and the other diplomatic negotiational. Hell! These pissy little C and C raids into Laos and Cambodia aren't enough. We need to invade the North. To quote von Clausewitz: 'Warfare is an extension of diplomacy.' Hey, I'd like to see us get real diplomatic here."

"We could always bomb them back into the stone age." Gerber winked.

"I think some Air Force general named LeMay might have already suggested that," countered Maxwell, wryly.

Just then the waiter approached, presented the check and stood at Maxwell's elbow. "I hope you enjoyed your meal," said the diminutive waiter in a subdued voice.

They all nodded in assent. Punctuating their approval, Dirty Shirt burped, farted and scratched the side of his nose.

Nonplussed, the waiter made a big show of looking at his wristwatch. "Oh, but I see it's getting late."

Gerber glanced at his own watch. "What do you mean late?" he asked. "It's barely after nine."

The waiter fidgeted. Quietly he said, "You should leave by ten."

"Why should we leave by ten?" asked Bocker.

The waiter leaned over and in a near whisper said, "Because that's when the VC come in to eat their lobster."

After paying the bill, Gerber, Maxwell and the others were back on the street, mumbling to themselves about discretion being the better part of valor when Bocker stopped in front of a bar and said, "Let's duck in here and have a smoke."

They were in the midst of the gin mills and sin parlors strung along 100 P Alley, Tu Do Street when they came upon a bright neon sign hanging above the battered doorway screaming Saigon Rose. Wire mesh hung over windows to keep VC agents and twelve-year-old girls from hurling grenades into the crowd of hookers and GIs.

Fetterman grabbed the wire mesh and shook it. He nodded, satisfied that it was sufficiently anchored to actually provide some protection. "While a place like this can't compare to the open-air amenities, it will do," he pronounced.

They all trooped in after him. Just inside the door a heavily made-up bar girl in a miniskirt held her delicate hand against Fetterman's chest and implored, "I rove you too much. You buy me tea. O-kay?"

Fetterman knew the tea was nothing more than colored water that cost the equivalent of a buck a shot. And the bar girls got a percentage of all the drinks they suckered GIs into buying. Fetterman wasn't a cheap Charley, but he wasn't stupid, either. Without a word, he pushed on past her.

Another bar girl wearing a bright yellow, wet-look minidress saw the men entering and called out in a singsong voice, "Herro, Maxwell. You want more boom-boom tonight?" She frowned and rubbed the inside of her calves. "Only this time you must take off those sirry green boots."

Maxwell's face flushed red. He ignored the woman and pushed on past her.

The woman in the yellow miniskirt turned to another heavily made-up woman standing next to her and held her thumb and forefinger barely an inch apart in a scathing appraisal of Maxwell's male dimensions.

The Gerber group took a table in the back corner with the jukebox on one side and a potted palm on the other. Fetterman patted its withered leaves as he sat down next to it. Maxwell ordered a round of beers. There was no American brew available, explained the waitress, so they drank the Vietnamese beer with the brand name of Ba Muoi Ba, which translated to Number 33.

Bocker held up the dark brown bottle, grimaced and aptly stated, "Ba Muoi Ba. Hands down, it is the world's worst beer."

"Made from the best formaldehyde money can buy," said Fetterman, with great seriousness. "Besides, drinking this swill saves time for the graves registration boys. They can send the bodies on to Oakland without embalming."

"Yankee ingenuity," joked Dirty Shirt. "Isn't that what this war is all about?"

After downing three beers each and listening to a dozen 45s blasting out of the speaker next to them, their numbed ears were no longer sensitive to the jukebox playing Rolling Stones music so loudly that you could recognize the song, but not quite make out the lyrics. In the middle of Mick Jagger's refrain, Fetterman nudged Gerber and pointed across the room.

Gerber looked up and saw a tall, slender, green-eyed woman staring in his direction. He felt a familiar jolt of electricity as their eyes met across the barroom. The lady was Robin Morrow, an attractive, intelligent woman he had had occasion to sleep with. But it was more than that. Or was it, he mused.

He had been afraid of this inevitable meeting and at the same time longed for contact with her. She took her time walking over to the table, but soon he felt her hand touch his. Suddenly he felt hot. It was too long since he had been in the company of a round-eyed woman, especially one whose treasures held a bittersweet flavor for him. "Shall we sit somewhere?" he said to her.

She nodded. He thought he detected a hint of a smile. Was she up to something, he wondered. Bocker winked at him. "Guess we'll catch up with you in the morning." Robin squeezed his arm.

Gerber nonchalantly motioned to an empty table. She nodded and they walked over to it. "What'll it be?" said the waiter.

"Whiskey, ice and water. Make it Beam's," she said, pulling a big wad of folded piasters out of her purse. "I'll buy."

After the waitress brought their drinks to the table, Robin downed hers in one healthy gulp. "I never told you this, but you drink like a man," said Gerber.

"So do you."

The tired air-conditioning unit wasn't keeping up with the wet tropical air, if it was even switched on, and the dank atmosphere of the Saigon Rose was clouded over with so much cigarette smoke that it was hard to breathe. Overhead, the ancient ceiling fan whirred, the big, flat wooden paddle blades circulating hot moist air around the room. The slight breeze it created raised the hairs up and down the back of Gerber's neck. All around him, off-duty American servicemen were getting roaring drunk, either trying to forget bloody firefights and dead buddies they'd never see again, or Department of the Army forms typed in triplicate.

Robin raised her glass to Gerber and nodded in a silent toast.

"What are we toasting?"

"Fate," she replied. "Simple fate."

Gerber remembered how it had all begun. During his first tour of duty in Vietnam he had met and fallen in love with Karen Morrow, Robin's sister. She was a dead ringer for Karen; the hair looked lighter, but the pose, the shoulders and the shape looked almost enough like her for her to be a twin. Gerber felt his stomach grow cold as he remembered his deeply felt pain when Karen, an Air Force nurse, had rotated back to the States. The wound was laid open again months later when he found out that Karen had lied to him. She was married and had been the whole time they had been sleeping together in Vietnam. She had never said a word about it. Gerber's distress was somewhat relieved by the acknowledgement that at least he wasn't the cuckolded husband back in the States. Regardless, the Karen Morrow affair had gotten to him more than he cared to acknowledge because he hadn't fallen in love with Karen, he had stepped in it.

And some months later in a Saigon bar, he recognized Karen, but when he approached the figure he saw the close resemblance. That had been the beginning of a quasi-love affair between himself and the woman who now sat at the table with him in a sleazy Saigon bar.

Sometimes in the middle of the night he found himself wondering whether that fortuitous meeting had been a gift from God or a cruel joke. He remembered the time when Robin had stripped on the stage of a downtown Saigon nightclub in an attempt to gain his attention. He recalled the time she had gotten drunk with his A-team after the battle for Hobo Woods. He remembered washing her back in the shower and seeing the thin network of scars crisscrossing her back from the beating she had endured at the hands of a sadistic Vietcong officer. But most of all he remembered how it aroused his emotions to kiss the nape of her neck and to sink into the warmth of her. In their scattered moments spent together, the two of them had shared plenty and yet remained strangers.

And now they sat across from each other at a table in a crowded Asian dive where he could smell the intoxicating blend of perspiration and her perfume. It was as if she were surrounded by a fragrant cloud enveloping everything near to her. Underneath the table, she delicately rubbed her thigh against his. She took his hand in hers. It was as if she were using the crush of the crowd to her advantage. She smiled captivatingly at him.

From across the room, a slightly intoxicated Fetterman caught Gerber's eye and then raised his glass toward the couple. Maxwell, Bocker and the others were deep in conversation, seemingly oblivious to their surroundings.

Gerber and Morrow drank for hours, talking about her career, Special Forces and their war. At one point, she swept her arm across the table to make a point and spilled drinks from several glasses. "I'm going into Cambodia," she said, her voice growing steadier as she spoke. "There's a story there I'm going to follow. I can't tell you much more than that. Jesus, now I'm beginning to sound like you furtive sneaky-Pete types. But when I get back from my little intrigue and you get back from yours, why don't you put in for R and R in Hong Kong or Bangkok? I'll meet you there."

"Exactly where are you going in Cambodia and who are you going with?" asked Gerber in a worried voice.

"Understand I can't tell you exactly where, but I can divulge that I'll be packing a rucksack and wearing boots. And I'll be safe enough, Jerry Maxwell is going too. He got me the boots, the new lightweight jungle boots."

"That man has the cunning of a warehouse rat." Gerber paused for a moment before he went on. "I don't mean to tell you your business, but don't you think wandering off into the jungle is a bit above and beyond your job description? My God, and with Maxwell at the helm you are very likely to get yourself killed. Not that it's any of my business."

She laid her warm hand on his forearm. "Look, Maxwell's not my first choice." She shrugged. "But right now he's my only connection. I'll admit the asshole's personality leaves a lot to be desired. After all, he graduated from Yale. While his peer group was involved in dating and back seat sex, learning life's necessary social skills, Jerry's nose was buried in his books. What else can you expect from an Ivy Leaguer?"

"His nose was buried somewhere, but I don't think you want to hear where. I'll give you a clue. It's still there."

"Listen, Mack, this is a good chance for a hot story and I'm going to take it. After all, you only live once."

He nodded. "Another way to say it is you only die once."

Undaunted, she took a big gulp from her drink and then pointed a finger at him. "This is the kind of war where you learn just about as much as you are able to believe. And I only believe what I see."

The long version of Eric Burdon singing "Sky Pilot" came to an end on the jukebox, and the hooting and hollering seemed to grow fully one hundred decibels louder, or enough to drown out the takeoff of a B-52 bomber. Somewhere across horizons of the dimly lit room an irate soul banged his fist against a table. Men howled in laughter. On the dance floor GIs and their Oriental girlfriends danced so closely together that their bellies rubbed together. One couple kissed long and passionately.

Gerber gazed into Robin's half-drunk, sparkling eyes. He drew her out of her chair and onto his lap and kissed her long and passionately. They threw their arms around each other, laughing and hugging tightly.

Smiling lewdly, she pushed him back and leaned toward him. She pulled at the top of her blouse, revealing some cleavage. "Drink up," she said, with noticeably slurred speech. She grabbed her purse and staggered to her feet. "Drink up."

ARM IN ARM, Gerber and Morrow walked the three blocks to the old French hotel. Once upstairs, Gerber guided Morrow to their room, unlocked the door and helped her inside. Their room at the Imperial was beautiful, with heavy plush curtains, a table, two deep armchairs and a big green bed. Gerber dropped into one of the chairs and began to unlace his boots. If it hadn't been for the occasional rattle of gunfire in the distance and the incessant swooshing of jet planes on their final approach to Tan Son Nhut air base, the two of them could have lived undisturbed in the fantasy that they were indeed in Paris, and not Saigon, South Vietnam.

As he finished kicking off his boots, he heard Morrow's shoes thud on the floor. He looked up to see her sitting on the edge of the bed, beckoning him with open arms. He stared at her blond hair, matted with sweat and clinging to her brow. He wanted to touch her, to kiss her, to ease the blouse from her shoulders and the skirt from her hips. But he didn't move.

She looked at her chest and began to unbutton her blouse. He helped her strip her blouse from her shoulders. Then she unfastened her skirt and stood to let it fall, revealing black panties and bra. Giggling like a schoolgirl she sat back on the bed.

Gerber felt a special fondness for her. So many civilians, and especially women, had never really been hungry or thirsty. Hadn't experienced war firsthand. He knew that even in Vietnam most of the soldiers had never seen combat. They might have heard the firing a mile or so away, but had never been mortared or shot at. Robin had. And many of the women Gerber had met were nothing but trouble. They talked in circles in an attempt to maximize their own attractiveness. Robin wasn't that way. She was a fairly straight shooter, who said what she thought and stood by what she said.

He moved toward her and gently pushed her shoulders, tipping her back on the bed. He undressed quickly, then positioned himself next to her. She lifted her pelvis and slipped off her underwear. She threw one leg across his body, finally lying on top of him. Her fingers traveled down his midriff, tangling themselves in his pubic hair, caressing him. In turn he stroked her hair, and alternately reached down to squeeze her buttocks. Her nipple hardened in his mouth and he nipped at it lightly. She cried out in passion.

She rocked backward, moaning and groaning. Her movements came faster and faster, then suddenly she clenched her jaw and cried out. He felt her shudder, then her body relaxed on top of him.

After a few minutes she came back to life and licked beads of sweat on his hairy chest. "That was nice," she purred.

Gerber felt her weight on top of him, felt her warmth, heard her breathing against his ear and knew everything was as it should be.

GERBER HEARD SOMEONE calling his name from a faraway place.

"Mack. Mack."

A shiver ran along his spine. Terror gripped his whole body. He didn't know where he was: North Vietnam, South Vietnam or Fort Bragg.

"Mack, are you awake?" Robin laid her head against his chest and tried to hear whether his breathing was regular.

He felt the sheets bunched up by his feet at the bottom of the bed and remembered he was with Robin Morrow. He pretended not to hear her calling his name.

"I know you're awake, Mack. I know you too well. You can't fool me." He nodded gingerly, opened his eyes and looked at her.

After that they sat in the darkened room for a long while. No words were exchanged. Finally she asked, "All those times we made love," she said, "here and at the Carasel Hotel. Did you ever close your eyes and pretend I was her? Wish that it was her and not me making love to you."

Gerber answered with a blank expression.

She smiled sweetly. "Karen. Did you ever pretend I was Karen?"

Gerber shook his head. "No. I'd never do that."

Robin went on. "She's free now. Single. He divorced her after he caught her with another man." Gerber was aware that Robin was carefully studying his face for any reaction at all.

He sighed. "I see. And so now you're wondering how this wonderful news about the dragon lady will influence me. Whether I will forsake you, the Army and the people of Vietnam just to beg milady Karen for one more chance. After all, the world stopped spinning ever since she stepped out of my life."

Robin shrugged. "I'm no fool. After all, more than once when we've been doing it you cried out her name in a moment of passion."

"I most certainly did not," he said with a grin.

"You're right. I'm sorry I said that. Of course you didn't. I hate myself for testing you. It's just that Karen is single now and we've reached a point where I want to know where I stand with you. Where we stand. Us. Our relationship."

Gerber wrinkled his face. "I hate that word."

"What word?" she said with a pained expression.

"The *R* word. You know, relationship."

"Oh," she said. "Your attitude toward all this tells me what I need to know about where I stand with you."

Gerber decided to let the topic of conversation die, if she would let it. It wasn't exactly the subject he felt comfortable with just before a big mission. After all, he had more important things to preoccupy himself with. Love-swooning males were poor risks in combat. It wasn't fair to himself, or to his men. Besides, he'd known for a long time that Karen was divorced. She'd written him with the news. He'd ignored it.

Robin took that moment to circle her arms around him and soon they were making love a second time.

6

MAC SOG ISOLATION COMPOUND NEAR TAN SON NHUT

The next morning, Gerber, Fetterman, Bocker, Dirty Shirt and the two tribesmen from the Central Highlands, Krung and Kai, sat in gray metal folding chairs at the front of the briefing room. The Americans all had steaming mugs of coffee in front of them, but the two Orientals sipped from cold bottles of Pepsi.

The space appeared virtually indistinguishable from any other briefing room they had ever been in. It didn't matter whether the concrete foundations had been poured in the soil of North Carolina, Germany, Panama, Okinawa or the republic of South Vietnam. If you had seen one, you had seen them all. The walls in all of these locations were adorned with the same government printing office artwork: essentially artistic impressions of U.S. Army battlefield victories. And as a tribute to someone's sense of reality, some battlefield losses were also portrayed; but only when the defeat had won eternal glory for the military when all of the men in the command had died valorously. If you were young and impressionable, and stared at the battle scene represented in vivid blue and red colors, it made your blood yearn for a posthumously awarded Medal of Honor.

Older wiser men, career soldiers, viewed the icons with a more sanguine eye, as monuments to brave men who had been in the wrong place at the wrong time, doing a job that civilians didn't have the heart for, and sometimes didn't appreciate.

At the front of the briefing room stood a wooden podium, a tripod for holding charts, a pull-down movie screen and a long table. On the back wall were two crossed AK-47s and a pair of bullet-ridden black pajamas with a sign underneath proclaiming the wearer as a hero of Khe Sanh. But most of the room was taken up by several rows of gray metal folding chairs.

Hurry up and wait, thought Gerber impatiently. Hurry up and wait. Trying to make himself more comfortable, he shifted his weight, and inadvertently grated his chair a fraction of an inch across the floor, scuffing the waxed finish and making a strange sound.

In the back of the room the PFC who sat next to the idling slide projector took a long drag on his cigarette and gave silent thanks that he wasn't assigned to a field unit like the poor bums sitting in front of him. He had seen a thousand such men come and go. He wondered how many of their bodies lay rotting in the jungles and paddies of Cambodia, Laos and North Vietnam.

Footsteps clattered behind Gerber and he craned his neck over his shoulder to see who had entered the room.

A Special Forces major with the beginnings of a paunch and graying temples walked to the front of the room with a manila folder clutched in one hand and a dull mat aluminum briefcase gripped in the other. There was a strange smile on his face.

Fetterman jabbed his elbow into Bocker's ribs and whispered, "I know him. I know that guy. The old-timer was with the Wehrmacht, in World War Two, been in SF since Christ was a private. A good man. He'd do to go on patrol with."

Fetterman had met the major, when the major had been but a captain, in a Tokyo bar back during the Korean conflict. Over what seemed like an oil drum full of sake, drunk from the traditional square wooden cups, the two men had warily swapped backgrounds and then became lifelong friends. That night a dumbfounded Fetterman had learned that eighteen-year-old Private Klaus Blauveldt had defended Omaha Beach during the Normandy invasion on the very day that Fetterman had been one of the attackers.

"The Americans died like flies," said Klaus, with a sake-thickened tongue, as he talked about D day. "In the bunkers the German soldiers were throwing up and bawling like babies. It made us sick to be killing so many brave men. They died like flies."

Fetterman remembered what it had been like to be pinned down on the sand, and to look around and see a dead body contorted in one position or another every six feet. He remembered the sinking feeling he had had in the pit of his stomach years after the war, when he had learned that the situation had looked so bad at one point that General Eisenhower had considered abandoning the beachhead.

But that was more than twenty years ago. And former enemies now wore the same uniform, served the same master and battled the same enemy. Fetterman wondered if in twenty years Americans and North Vietnamese would enjoy a similarly amicable relationship. Not very likely, he thought, a trace of anger welling up inside him. Not likely at all.

The major stood at the front of the room, laid his folder down on the table and faced his audience. "Good morning, gentlemen, I am Major Blauveldt and this briefing is classified Secret." He spoke with a slight German accent.

Gerber pumped the button on his black, U.S. government ballpoint pen, poised it over his yellow ruled notepad and wondered what he was about to hear.

Blauveldt nodded imperceptibly at Fetterman, then looked directly at Gerber. "Your area of operations will be located near Phu Tho, North Vietnam, roughly sixty miles northwest of Hanoi." Blauveldt nodded to the soldier in the back of the room. The lights went out and the projector blinked on, bathing the dark room in hazy blue light.

Blauveldt's voice pierced the darkness. "After you see the Intel we have for you here today, you'll appreciate why Jerry Maxwell delayed this briefing for twenty-four hours. A month ago while on a routine sweep a squad from the Big Red One grabbed a seventeen-year-old girl. Seems the Commie organizers outside of Hanoi persuaded this kid and fifty other high school boys and girls to pick up AK-47s and spend their vacation liberating the South. Unfortunately for them and their loved ones there won't ever be a class reunion. A Cobra gunship minigunned them, wiped out the kids and their NVA cadre. Needless to say, after the mind-bending experts at the POW center outside of Bien Hoa finished interrogating the sole survivor, we have firsthand knowledge of the military movements in and around her hometown, Phu Tho, North Vietnam."

Gerber pursed his lips. "How do you rate the accuracy of what she told you."

"Very reliable. We strapped a lie detector to her arm the whole time. Whether or not the machine intimidated her into telling the truth or not, we don't know, of course. But what she did blab to us backs up our other intel, the recon photos and the agents in place."

The major called for the next image and the slide projector clicked, illuminating the silver screen with an aerial photo of a radio transmitting site. With his black shadow intruding on the picture, Blauveldt touched his pointer to the center of the screen to focus attention on a tall radio antenna. "Here is your first landmark. It's a CW station, about a thousand watts, or so the experts tell us."

Bocker recognized the reconnaissance photo as the kind taken by high-altitude SR-71s. "So our mission is to knock out the transmitter."

"Wrong," said the major good-naturedly. "Hit the lights, will you, PFC."

The overhead lights lit up the room. Blauveldt, Gerber and the rest blinked for a moment before their eyes adjusted to the illumination and then the major unfolded a map and spread it across the expanse of a long gray metal table. He cleared his throat, the signal for the team to leave their chairs and crowd around him. He pointed to the map and gave commentary; they listened carefully, not wanting to miss any part of it. They all knew that more than one of the spike teams had mysteriously disappeared from the face of the earth. And none of Gerber's men wanted to join the swollen ranks of Krung's ghost army.

Blauveldt swept his hand across the breadth of the map. "From dawn to dusk, nothing moves south of

Hanoi all the way to the DMZ. The highways are deserted and the bridges are knocked out. It's been weeks since the Navy pilots off the carriers have spotted daytime traffic. North Vietnam's railroads are virtually shut down. All of the rail bridges have been knocked out. One by one we're hitting their locomotives.

"By night their truck convoys, consisting of groups of four to ten Russian Zils and Czechoslovakian Skodas, stick to the back roads. When they hear planes, they blackout their headlights and haul ass to the nearest village." Blauveldt's face took on a sour expression. "They've figured out we're avoiding civilian targets. Crever ferrows," he said wryly.

Gerber pumped his black ballpoint pen. "You said the bridges were out. How are the trucks crossing water obstacles?"

Blauveldt replied with a tight grin. "Ferries. Essentially sampans lashed together, carrying one truck across the water at a time. Still, they're easy to spot. You look for where a road goes down to the river on one side and comes out on the other." He shrugged, "We're knocking out two and three boats a night."

Blauveldt opened a manila folder and took out an eight-by-ten glossy black-and-white photograph of an Oriental girl. He handed the full-length picture to Gerber. "This is Thuy Thien, the seventeen-year-old school kid I told you about."

Gerber gave a low whistle. "Not bad."

"For a slope," added Dirty Shirt. Krung jabbed him in the ribs.

Without a word Blauveldt handed Gerber a dog tag for someone named O'Hanlon, Regular Army, a Roman Catholic with blood type O-Positive. After Gerber had a few moments to study the ID, Blauveldt went on with the briefing.

"She had that little item in her pocket when we picked her up," said Blauveldt. "We did some checking and discovered that PFC O'Hanlon was a straight-leg KIA as of about a week ago. Incidentally, he was put in for a Bronze Star for Valor. He was manning a machine gun covering his unit's withdrawal up on the Laotian border near Lang Vei."

Gerber handed the dog tag to Fetterman, and then asked the major, "How'd she get it? She kill O'Hanlon and take his dog tag as a war trophy? What's the significance of her having it in her possession as it relates to our mission?"

Blauveldt shrugged. "It's all just part of the package. Maybe she killed him, maybe she didn't. At this point it really doesn't matter. Like I said, she was very cooperative on the intel side. Her interview with S-2 confirms the interpretation of the recon photos like the one of the radio site I just showed you. It all adds up to the fact that Phu Tho is a staging area with a very big ammo dump. That's why I showed you the radio site. It's a mile down the road from the ammo dump."

Gerber, Bocker and the rest of the men studied the map, the photo of the girl, Thuy Thien, and the photo of the radio transmitter.

Gerber was beginning to get a handle on the situation presented to them. "So our mission is to infiltrate and bring back the coordinates so the Air Force can fly over some B-52s and drop some iron bombs without causing any more civilian casualties than necessary. That's the mission, right?"

"Wrong. We want you to infiltrate and plant some tulips."

Gerber and Fetterman looked at each other, wondering whether the strange affliction that had influenced Maxwell was contagious.

"Tulips," said Gerber in a carefully measured voice.

Blauveldt shook his head. "I didn't say flowers, I said tulips. It's new technology, electronic sensors that detect if anyone is tiptoeing through the tulips. Get it?" Blauveldt picked up the aluminum briefcase from the floor, laid it flat on the table and opened the lid. He pulled out a black spike with a knob on the end and held it up in front of them. "As you can see they resemble tulips, sort of. The wizards refer to them as seismic geophones. Seismic intrusion detectors. We call 'em SID for short. SID is sensitive enough to feel a human being walking in the jungle up to three hundred feet away. Trucks lay down a bigger footprint so the tulips can detect a truck on the roll within one thousand. The batteries hold a charge for six months." Blauveldt passed the SID around the room.

Gerber stroked his chin with one hand and held a SID in the other. With a weight that closely matched that of a white phosphorous hand grenade, the black device approximated the size of a Pepsi bottle. The knob on the big end was only a little smaller than a tennis ball, the rest of the sensor was spike-shaped to ease its planting in the ground.

"Let me guess the rest of the scenario," said Gerber. "Some spooks sit in a commo van down by the DMZ and monitor the telemetry these gizmos put out."

"Well, yeah, sort of. That explanation is close enough for government work. Regardless, with these sensors planted along key trails, we know where and when the troop movements are on the move even in bad weather. With the precise targeting data we get from SID the Air

Force's FAC and her family of Phantoms can roar in and kick the shit out of Charlie and company. By the way, the SIDs are really helping out up in Khe Sanh. In fact two enemy divisions were so badly battered by bombing raids that they had to pull back into Laos for regrouping."

"Sounds too easy," said Gerber. "All we got to do is infiltrate North Vietnam with a bunch of electronic gear and plant a patch of tulips so the intelligence analysts can monitor the infiltration routes into the South."

Blauveldt nodded. "All you have to do is plant twelve of them in the spots we designate. As easy as spring planting in the garden in front of an English cottage. It's that simple."

"Sounds good to me," said Gerber. "Too easy."

Blauveldt held up a finger. "There is just one more thing," he said with a mischievous glint in his eye.

Bocker rolled his eyes back. Fetterman swatted him in mock seriousness.

"What's this one more thing?" asked Gerber.

"Don't worry. This is the good part. You'll like it." Blauveldt reached once more into the depths of the aluminum briefcase and came out with a little box the size of a school kid's lunch box. It was painted flat black so no light would reflect off its surface. "You'll deploy with a new piece of radio gear." Blauveldt screwed a short, whip antenna into the top of the device, then pointed out the field strength meter and frequency tuning dial. "This new goodie will provide you with real-time intelligence data that may save your life. One man on your team will be trained to use it. His job will be to monitor the NVA militia frequencies. Naturally this should be someone who speaks Vietnamese. And more important, it should be someone who's familiar with the northern dialect. It does sound somewhat different, even more singsongy than our esteemed colleagues here in the south. Closer to Chinese."

"I get it," said Bocker. "So if the VC start talking about being close to some Americans in the boondocks, we'll hear their radio traffic and we can *di di mau*."

"Roger that. *Di di mau* most ricky tick."

Dirty Shirt sighed. "I guess I'm it. I speak Vietnamese the best. Attended the Defense Language Institute in Monterey for twelve weeks." He took the little radio out of Blauveldt's hands and immediately thumped it on its side. It echoed back hollowly.

Blauveldt cleared his throat.

Oblivious to the subtle warning, Dirty Shirt thumped it again. "Hmm," he said as he held it against his ear. The expression on his face looked as if he believed he could divine its contents by merely thumping and listening, thumping and listening.

Blauveldt stood with his hands on his hips and a big frown.

Still oblivious to the major's stern looks of disapproval, Dirty Shirt twirled the little black knob up and down the frequency band.

Blauveldt cleared his throat and held out his outstretched hand. "Give it to me."

Dirty Shirt's face turned red as he nodded and handed over the miniature receiver.

Blauveldt grunted and handed the unit to Gerber. "From this moment on," said Blauveldt, "consider yourselves in isolation."

Gerber nodded. Being in isolation meant no contact with the outside world. That way, a mission wouldn't be inadvertently compromised or deliberately betrayed by one of the men assigned to it. Now that they were in isolation, Gerber and Bocker and the rest could get down to the nitty-gritty and determine exactly what equipment to bring with them, whether to infiltrate by land or air, how to execute the mission and exfiltrate.

Blauveldt went on. "I'll function as your AST. Anything you need in the way of resources, be it rucksacks, weapons, intel or whatever, you'll channel through me. You know the routine," he said. "You've been in isolation more times than you've been laid." He paused for a moment, then added, "Except for you, Dirty Shirt. I doubt you've ever been laid."

GERBER AND FETTERMAN planned the intricate details of their mission into North Vietnam. With the topographical map spread wide across the tabletop, the two men leaned over the map and intently studied the cartography. Superimposed on its blues, greens and browns were looping ridge lines that described the jungle-covered mountains and flooded rice fields.

With his beret into his jungle fatigue pants pocket, Gerber studied the Red River, the Song Hong Ha that cut squarely through their area of operations. Sometimes called Mother River, the inland waterway began in the south China province of Yunnan and curved southeasterly through the rice paddies and rain forests. Then the Red River Valley made a wide bend to the south just before Phu Tho. Gerber noticed how the waters dipped and curved again at Son Tay, then straightened and flowed on through the center of Hanoi, to the delta and on out to the Gulf of Tonkin and the South China Sea.

It was a good map, thought Gerber, prepared by the Army Map Service only a couple of years before, and therefore the Special Forces captain deemed it to be accurate. The map showed the Phu Tho area in great detail, pinpointing the exact location of individual rice paddies, temples, pagodas, farmers' hootches, roads, pathways through the rain forest and even an abandoned airstrip built by the French before the fall of Dien Bien Phu.

The airstrip stood out because its runway was located next to the radio site Blauveldt had shown them. In his mind's eye, Gerber could clearly see the squares of brown paddies in the lowlands separated by green, grassy dikes. And at the edge of the rice fields, the ground sloped upward into the tropical rain forest.

In essence this was the type of terrain that they knew very well from their dozens of patrols and covert operations. Brow furrowed, Gerber considered and eliminated the possibilities for a drop zone: tropical rain forests, rice paddies, little used roads. He told Fetterman, "We could HALO in, B-52 out of Udorn like we did before. That would be the best bet because we could mask our infiltration route by accompanying B-52s on a raid. We'd just exit the aircraft before they got to their target."

"Ubon would be closer to Phu Tho, cut down on our flight time and we wouldn't be as worn out by the time we got on the ground."

Gerber shook his head. "No. The runway's too narrow at Ubon. Those wheels that hold up the wings on takeoff would be dragging in the dirt. We could land one there but it would never take off again."

Dirty Shirt approached them with a sheet of paper and stood a couple of paces away and listened to them talk. He was biding his time for the right moment to talk with Gerber. When he heard the topic of HALO his ears perked up. "Got a problem with that method of insertion, Captain Gerber. I'm not HALO qualified," he said, grimacing.

Gerber looked at him quizzically.

Dirty Shirt gave a sheepish grin. "Hey, I've earned Viet jump wings, SAS jump wings and Nicaraguan jump wings. I'm a master blaster. I applied for HALO school, but my eyes weren't good enough to pass the flight physical. I'm not close enough to twenty-twenty vision."

"Fuck," said Gerber flatly. "That means we're stuck contour-flying in a C-130 for three hundred-odd miles. Not exactly my idea of a comfortable ride. And every rice-farming VC in the world is going to hear us coming all the way from the 17th parallel."

"The pilot will love it," said Fetterman. "I can already see the flight crew rubbing their hands together and shouting in glee, 'Oh, boy. We get to fly down in the dirt. We get to fly in the dirt.' They're funny like that. They like it when they get to break regulations."

"I can relate to that," said Dirty Shirt.

Fetterman hunched over the map and jabbed the area west of Phu Tho with his pencil. "More sparsely populated over here. We could still swing in from Laos and effectively minimize the number of hostile population who might hear or see us. Hear no evil, see no evil, speak no evil."

Gerber nodded. "The idea has a certain merit." Pointing at the map, Gerber showed Bocker their target—a highway on the outskirts of Phu Tho. Along both the ditches paralleling the road they would sow the electronic tulips that would then monitor the traffic on the highway. "Here's where Blauveldt wants us to plant the listening devices. And since we want to be inserted as close to the target as possible, it seems obvious we'll use the rice paddies for a drop zone.''

Fetterman nodded. ''I figure. Yeah, it's dry season. Otherwise we'd have to chance straddling a branch during a tree landing or drowning in a flooded field.'' Fetterman's fingers traced the waterways. ''In all seriousness we could attempt a water landing into the Red River or one of these canals.''

Gerber tapped the map. ''Right here. Where the tree line meets the rice paddies. We can use the highway to the south as a reference point when we exit the aircraft. With the moon full, it'll reflect off the pavement and the Red River. This is our drop zone, right here.''

''Yeah, I see it,'' said Fetterman.

''It'll do,'' agreed Bocker.

Gerber spoke directly to Sergeant Fetterman. ''You'll function as the jumpmaster on this drop, Tony,'' said Gerber as he laid a steel ruler across the map and measured the distance from the drop zone to the river. ''We'll infiltrate on the far side of the mountain, using it for cover, and follow the ridge line around to the other side. It's not far. A mile at the most.''

Holding up the typewritten sheet of paper for Gerber to see, Dirty Shirt closed the distance between himself and the map table. ''Here's our radio call signs, frequencies and commo schedule.''

''Simplex or duplex?'' asked Bocker, taking the sheet of paper and quickly glancing at it before he handed it to Gerber.

''Duplex,'' responded Dirty Shirt. ''We'll send Morse code on one frequency, net control will answer our transmission on another. That'll keep the little bastards guessing.''

Gerber examined the sheet of paper. "You know the routine, memorize this and then destroy it per Army regulations. We don't want this mission compromised because some gook with VC ties sifts through MACV garbage and gets lucky."

Dirty Shirt grinned as he touched his forefinger to his temple. "Already done. Burned indelibly into my memory. Why, I'll be able to tell my grandkids all of the salient details of this gallant mission into the jaws of death."

"As long as they all have clearances, Shirt, and have a need to know," joked Gerber. He was in a whimsical mood because the mission was coming together well. It boded well for their success.

Fetterman cleared his throat. "Ah, what about weapons? We going to bring any?"

"Hey, how about grease guns?" said Gerber. "Good cyclic rate of fire, good for keeping heads down. Any objections, Sergeant Fetterman?"

Dirty Shirt groaned. "Good weapon, yeah, I suppose, but the goddamn ammo is too heavy. Two 30-round magazines weigh damn near as much as an M-16."

Fetterman waved him off good-naturedly. "Relax. It's an inside joke between me and the captain. He knows I'm partial to the M-3. The captain's just being funny." With that, Fetterman turned to Gerber. "With AKs we can infiltrate with a basic load and scrounge ammo as we go. Let the Commies be our ammo bearers."

Gerber agreed. "AK-47s it is. Specify Russian-made to Blauveldt, tell him we won't accept any of the Chinese junk. Same with ammo, it's got to be Russian or Czechoslovakian. And as for the rest of the equipment, we're going to need to move fast once we're on the ground. Get in. Get out. That means pack light. I want us infiltrated and extracted in less than twenty-four hours. We'll run on the edge of hungry. Just carry water, weapons and one radio. An empty belly will help keep us alert.''

"I like that idea,'' added Dirty Shirt. "Run on the edge of hungry. Almost sounds like the sage advice you'd hear at one of the Buddhist temples. Though I suppose the night before we jump off we could gorge ourselves and fill our bellies like buffalo hunters after a big kill. No sense burdening ourselves with food and other nonessentials that would just weigh us down. Besides, we'll only be out one night anyway.''

"Commo though,'' said Bocker, gritting his teeth. "I'd like it better if we humped two radios and two sets of batteries. Commo has always been the weak link in these behind-the-lines missions. With one radio, if a circuit board or other electronic component gives up the ghost, we can't give a shout for the exfiltrate. With a backup along, we're covered.''

"Count yourself fortunate we're taking any radio at all,'' said Gerber. "Some teams infiltrate without any radios and go out by prearranged LZ and extraction times.''

"If we bring two radios what about the extra weight?'' asked Fetterman.

"I can carry it, I'll be light,'' said Dirty Shirt. "I'd see it as a sound investment in my future. Besides, like I said, I'll be light anyway.''

"How's that?'' asked Bocker suspiciously.

"I won't have a jungle hammock.''

"How's that?''

"Don't sleep in 'em. Don't trust them.''

"Why not?''

"Malaya. Ten or so years ago. My partner got kilt one night. Couldn't get out of his hammock in time. Zipper stuck."

"Communist guerrillas light him up?"

"Nope. Got squashed."

"This is a joke, right?"

"We had set up camp near a wild elephant trail. At midnight the pachyderms came stumbling through and knocked over a tree onto him, squashed him flat. Never forgot the look of him lying there with his tongue hanging out. Looked like a road kill."

"Oh." The others pondered whether or not they'd bring jungle hammocks this trip.

"I'll say it one more time," said Gerber. "We'll bring just one radio and take our chances. And nobody is packing a jungle hammock. We don't want to get too comfortable. We can't afford any extra weight dragging us down. Speed and maneuverability will be essential."

"What about targets of opportunity?" said Fetterman. "Might be kind of nice to bring some blocks of C-4 in case we see anything we might like to blow up. Maybe we could sneak in and save the Air Force the time and trouble. I mean, after all, we'll be in the neighborhood anyway."

"Yeah," said Bocker. "I don't like the idea of all this sneaking around without being able to reduce the overpopulation in the North. I think they could use our help."

Gerber agreed. "We'll carry claymores. That way we can use them as defensive weapons, or extract the C-4 out of them for demo. Each man carries one. Bocker and I will carry the detonators."

Everyone knew that separating the detonators from the explosive charges was a time-honored safety precaution, so that if a bullet hit a detonator, it wouldn't go off and detonate all of the explosives. Further, dividing the detonators between two men improved the odds that at least one man would survive and make it to the target with the detonators intact.

Gerber went on, "To make up for the weight on the guys carrying claymores, Fetterman and I will carry the batteries for the radio."

ONCE THE EQUIPMENT list was written up, they requisitioned the necessary items from Blauveldt, who delivered it a short while later. Then the team busied themselves with dividing up the twelve SIDs, the claymores and the radio gear among the rucksacks. Off to one side of his men, Gerber sat on the floor, stripping the adhesive tape off a black cardboard tube. That done, he took off its top, pulled out an M-26 hand grenade and hung it on his webgear. He did the same to another tube, but before hanging the grenade on his belt, he held it for a moment in the palm of his hand.

He sat with his legs crossed, studying the squat green body and the pin with the pulling ring that started the five-second delay fuse burning its way clear to the detonating charge. Staring at the olive drab grenade in his hand, Gerber found himself wondering how he came to be in the company of men who felt so much at home amid the heat of battle.

In preparation for the covert action mission, Bocker was the first to take his turn reading the United States Army Area Handbook for Vietnam. It was standard operating procedure for any A-team to assemble an area study before infiltrating the operational area. Bocker knew how important it was to understand the big picture, including geographic characteristics of the region as well as the population, the indigenous language and the customs.

Once he finished with the book he went on to read a recent CIA report on the province. Halfway into it, Bocker gave a low whistle, "Found some interesting stuff here. Local militia major named Bao Dai. Bad fucker. Our assets in the North report that he likes to capture downed American pilots and do nasty things to them. Boy, if we have the opportunity, I'd like to off this son of a bitch." He handed the report to Gerber and showed him where to begin reading. Halfway through the page he stiffened and looked up at Bocker. Bocker nodded.

"We may just have to find the time to drop in for tea," said Gerber. "This guy is begging for special attention."

"Speaking of assets and double agents and other intrigues, is there a safehouse we should know about?" asked Dirty Shirt.

Gerber grimaced. "'Fraid not. We're having a hell of a time keeping indigenous agents alive in the North. The only logistical support we'll have will be what we carry in on our backs. Naturally we can radio the SFOB and requisition items for airdrop. But if we do have to resort to that we'll run the attendant risks of detection when we key the transmitter. Their intercept operators might pick up our broadcast on a routine frequency sweep. We wouldn't want that."

Bocker joined in on the conversation. "Well, we've got to have commo with the SFOB to coordinate extraction. We're bringing a CW burst device, that will cut down on the length of our transmission time. Odds are good to middling they'll never even hear us on the air, much less have enough time to run a DF on us."

Gerber's face took on a stern demeanor and his voice was very sober. ''There's something we need to talk about. If anyone is captured. Talk. Tell them anything you want to. Lie or tell the truth. Either way it doesn't matter. Because if anyone is caught we're going to figure on the worst possible case, that you've talked and compromised the mission. We'll change the plans in midstream. In short, do whatever you need to do to minimize the torture, the pain. It's your call.''

7

FLIGHT LINE, TAN SON NHUT AIR BASE

A moon-bright sky washed down on Tan Son Nhut Air Base and the camouflaged C-123 that squatted on the pavement in front of the hangar. A yellow-tipped propeller began to rotate slowly as the pilot cranked the port engine. The radial power plant sputtered, coughed, then caught, blowing a column of black oily smoke out the exhaust ports. Starting to run clean, the engine thrummed with fine-tuned rhythm.

Gerber's kill team trooped up the loading ramp and into the plane, lugging rucksacks and rifles just as the pilot started the starboard engine. Now inside the aircraft, Gerber sat in the aluminum and nylon-webbed troop seat, pulled the seat belt across his lap and hooked it. The loadmaster walked along, handing out throwaway earplugs from a gallon plastic jar. Sitting on the ground in Saigon with the doors open and the ramp down, the heat and humidity were nearly insufferable.

Moments later the pilot taxied to the edge of the runway, locked the brakes and throttled up the engines to takeoff RPM. With both engines at full bore, the tips of the props blurred, the plane strained to leap forward.

The pilot released the brakes and slowly the aircraft picked up speed as it began its roll down the runway. The tires tick-ticked as they crossed the cracks in the pavement, the tick-ticks coming faster and faster. The pilot pulled back on the yoke, at one thousand feet he leveled off and pointed the nose of the plane toward North Vietnam.

On board, a few of the men seemed solemn faced and self-occupied; a couple seemed cheerful enough. Dirty Shirt stared out the aircraft portholes and watched the Pratt and Whitney twelve-cylinder radial churn blue exhaust flames around the cowling. The hypnotic colors took his mind off the parachute jump he would soon be making. Static line jumps always made him nervous.

Sitting immediately next to him was Gerber, his sweat-sodden jungle fatigues clinging to his back. Eyes closed, but fully alert, Gerber visualized every phase of the operation, trying to think of a snag that might come up. He weighed the chances for success. And failure. If the Air Force put them out over the right drop zone and everyone got onto the ground without injury, and if they could plant the electronic listening devices without being detected, they stood an excellent chance of making it to the LZ alive. But from the time they left the aircraft to the time they touched down again at Tan Son Nhut, a million things could go wrong.

The problem was that since you never knew what was going to go awry, there was no way to plan solutions until you were in the middle of it. And then you had better be a quick study, because it all came down very quickly when you were hundreds of klicks behind enemy lines.

Dirty Shirt shouted above the roar of the engines. "What altitude you say we're jumping from?"

"Five hundred feet," Gerber shouted back. "Five hundred feet."

Across the aisle Fetterman was a happy man. At the last minute Blauveldt had procured for him a virgin M-3A1 submachine gun packed in Cosmoline and wrapped in the original protective paper and tinfoil envelope. In its twenty-year life span, it hadn't been opened since it was sealed at the factory.

Fetterman sighed as he unscrewed the oilcan from the grip of his M-3A1, then fieldstripped his dull gray weapon to clean and oil it just one more time before infiltration. With the pieces balanced in his lap, he dabbed the bolt, guide rods and firing mechanism with a silicone cleaning cloth. Not too much oil, not too little. Then Fetterman reassembled the submachine gun and rubbed the rag across the length and breadth of its Parkerized finish.

Rather wryly he had noticed the name of the manufacturer stamped on the receiver: Champion Spark Plug Company, Cleveland, Ohio. And the serial number was 0012892. He found himself wondering why they had bothered using the double zeroes. No matter. Then he smiled in remembrance. During the Korean War they had captured several thousand Chinese-made rifles, with serial numbers registering in the millions. That had unnerved the S-2 types, who shuddered at the thought of untotaled millions of rifles in the hands of fanatical red Communists. In the end they decided that stamping all of those rifles with the big serial numbers didn't mean anything at all. Or so they hoped.

Satisfied with his own weapon's state of readiness, Fetterman slapped in place the blue-steel magazine, filled with thirty .45-caliber rounds. He stowed the cleaning rag, leaned back, closed his eyes and went to sleep.

Next to him Bocker sat silently with his arms folded across his chest, staring at the bulkhead across the aisle from him. Above Gerber's head and snapped at strategic intervals along the length of the aircraft were first-aid kits with red crosses emblazoned across a white background. Bocker knew from his experiences earlier in the war that the kits used to contain morphine, but when the narcotic ampoules and syringes inexplicably started disappearing, the painkilling drug was removed from the kit bags.

It was common knowledge that the denuded kits were no more potent than a suburban housewife's medicine cabinet, stuffed to overflowing with bandages, adhesive tape, antibiotic ointments, scissors and iodine. But Bocker knew about the chocolate-flavored survival candy bar laced with nuts, raisins and amphetamines that was tucked away in the back behind the sterile dressing. Bocker's eyes met Gerber's. His surreptitious gaze swept to the first-aid kit, then to Gerber, back to the first-aid kit and then finally back to Gerber.

Gerber looked up over his head to see what Bocker was trying to draw his attention to. Gerber nodded. Bocker smiled.

In the tail section of the plane, the red-haired crew chief, with a yellow pencil jutting out the pocket of his blue-green flight suit, sat on the stack of T-10 parachutes. These canopies were standard for static line jumps. The crew chief cupped his hands over his earphones to hear better over the roar of the engines. After a couple of moments nodding at whatever it was the pilot said to him, he peeled off the earphones and shouted to Gerber, "Ten minutes."

The team got to their feet, stretching stiff arms and leg muscles. Bocker cracked his knuckles. Fetterman yawned. One by one the men picked up a parachute and lugged it back to their troop seat.

Bocker hiked his rig onto his back as if it was an over-size rucksack, and wiggled his shoulders to get it to drop in place. That done, he adjusted the leg and chest straps, then fastened the lock plate that spread across his chest. When he was chuted up, the tight harness made him hunch over like an old man.

For the twentieth time during the flight from Tan Son Nhut to the drop zone, Dirty Shirt asked Gerber, "What altitude you say we're jumping from?"

"Five hundred feet," said Gerber patiently.

"I hate parachutes," said Dirty Shirt, fingering the empty D-ring on his harness.

"Say what?" asked the captain, cupping a hand over his ear.

"Said I love airborne operations." Gerber nodded and went back to his own thoughts.

Shirt sighed. They weren't wearing reserve chutes, because with only five hundred feet to free-fall, if the main canopy failed there wouldn't be enough for a re-serve chute to deploy and inflate. An unlucky jumper would crash and burn.

Below the plane rolled a carpet of treetops; the can-opy was like a bushy meadow suspended in thin air by one hundred-foot-tall trees. On the ground wild ani-mals roamed the mangrove swamps and mountain passes. Searching for prey, tigers howled to mark their territory and hungry snakes slithered among the twisty tree vines, waiting to drop down on unsuspecting warm-blooded mammals that were small enough to fit down their narrow throats.

Darkness, avionics and fancy flying hid the cargo plane's flight from the green glowing blips of the radar screens and the blinding flash of the surface-to-air missiles.

As the jungle terrain plunged into valleys and rose with hills, so dipped and rose the C-123. The manual called it contour flying. The pilot considered it stressful and dangerous, even with fancy instruments to rely upon. Silently, he caught himself wondering how many branches and leaves would shred if a prop chewed into a tree limb.

EARLY IN THE MORNING the convoy of four trucks had left the docks at Haiphong harbor and driven all day. The trucks were fitted with a crude, umbrellalike contraption consisting of a steel pipe frame with freshly cut tree branches hanging down over the sides. That helped reduce the possibility of a roving American fighter plane spotting them and opening fire. Just before nightfall, the big two-and-a-half-ton Russian ZIL 157s pulled off the road and formed a half circle.

With tired backs, the North Vietnamese regulars huddled around the little cook fire. It was built with a mat placed some inches above to hide the flames from the fighter planes that circled overhead like vultures. In the darkness, the flames licked crimson patterns on the soldiers' dark green uniforms. In quiet resignation, they slapped at the annoying bites and nibbles of tiny, nocturnal flying creatures.

Bao Dai sat on his heels in a wide-legged squat with his AK-47 rifle slung over his shoulder. With his porcelain bowl grasped in one hand he scooped handfuls of rice, devoid of salt or meat, into his mouth with the other. Bao was a one-eyed NVA officer, a short stocky man with a stubborn face, who had been born and raised in Hanoi.

Bao used moments like these to recall the good old days growing up near Thong Nhot, the beautiful lake surrounded by a garden in the center of Hanoi. In his late teens he had met a pretty girl, wearing a blue blouse and black trousers, in front of the thousand-year-old Mot Cot pagoda and courted her by the edge of the water. This was a predictable outcome, considering their age. For their honeymoon, he and Thanh had taken a room in the Ton Nhat Hotel on Kham Tien Street, the most popular hotel in Hanoi, where the two of them made love as only newlyweds can do. Bao smiled now, remembering the day that Thanh had given him the news of her pregnancy. Their first son, Huan, was born nine months later.

A slight breeze struck Bao's face, breaking his reverie, and his smile turned into a frown. He and his beautiful wife had lived on Phuc Tan Street. One day as he was returning from work, and not far from his home, he had heard the air raid sentry fire warning shots. Bao could hear the eerie sound of the bombs swooshing down from the heavens. Because the B-52s flew so high, it took a long time for the bombs to fall and there was plenty of time for him to run for a shelter. After the horrible noise abated and the ground stopped heaving, he ran for home. Short of breath, he surveyed the damage; his neighborhood was cratered like a lunar landscape.

Bao and Thanh's home had been one of the three hundred houses obliterated by the B-52 bombing raid. The officials who supervised the rescues broke the news to him. They had found his wife, his little boy and girl.

But the three of them were dead. Bao had witnessed the charred, burned foliage, and could still smell the horrible odor of the maimed, smoking bodies strewn across the wreckage of what had once been homes. He would never forget the look of blood still wet and dripping from his wife's body. Bao vowed that he would never forget the bomb craters, or what the Americans had done to his family. Bao rocked back on his heels and stared into the flames. It would be two years on May 19, on Ho Chi Minh's birthday. It seemed like a lifetime ago that he had lost his family.

Shortly after the bombing raid, Bao had enlisted in the Quan Doi Nan Dan, the People's Army of Vietnam, and completed officers' school at Son Tay, west of Hanoi.

These days he lived in the country where he trained soldiers to go south to help the Viet Nam Cong San, the VC. The majority of the Regional Forces trainees came into the army during the Three Readies Drive, when men volunteered that they were ready to fight, ready to join the army and ready to go wherever needed. Most often they were needed in the South. Bao himself had spent many months there with his comrades. Recently he had convinced an entire high school class to journey south and assist in the liberation. He wondered how they were doing, especially his beloved niece, Thuy Thien.

A voice piped up from the circle gathered around the camp fire. "Tell us, Bao. What is it like to fight in the south?"

"Yes," said another aspiring warrior. "What is it like to fight the Americans?"

The student soldiers could see the reflection of the camp fire in his eyes as he spoke. "It's like a grasshopper fighting an elephant," he said rather matter-of-factly. "The Americans lunge and plunge around not even knowing what's stinging them. And then after five or ten minutes we fade out."

"Oh, that would be frustrating," said one young voice. "They must go mad."

Bao Dai nodded. "Yes. From my hiding place I have seen half an American patrol wiped out without them seeing any one of us. Sometimes they weep with frustration and anger." Bao was silent for a few moments as he remembered various battles and American faces screaming in death. In his mind's eye he could plainly see the face of each of the U.S. soldiers he had killed.

"What about artillery and air strikes when the B-52s drop bombs on our bunkers and tunnels down south."

Bao spoke in a near monotone. "We dig deep. The bombs don't hurt as much as you think." Bao recounted tales of famous NVA victories, and his admirers listened until they all heard the sound. It began as a low rumbling far off in the mountains. Bao wasn't sure at first, but it was reminiscent of a sound he knew all too well: an airplane.

"Do you hear that?" said one.

Bao interrupted. "Ssssh . . . Listen," he said impatiently. Ear cocked toward the sky, he listened intently as the droning got louder.

"Shall we call the garrison?" asked a dark face.

Bao shook his head. "No need. This time." It was an airplane, but not an American B-52 bomber, he was certain of that. In fact it was probably one of their own, a North Vietnamese Air Force cargo plane on final approach for the base at Phuc Yen. Bao got to his feet and scanned the night sky for the landing lights. Unable to see it, he could hear its engines quite clearly. Yes, he mused, it was very likely another cargo plane on its way to Phuc Yen from China.

Just then the plane swung low overhead. To Bao it seemed barely above the treetops, its black shadow outlined by the flickering of bluish exhaust flames. The very earth seemed to tremble beneath his feet. And as quickly as it had come the sound of the plane faded away. Walking after it, Bao searched the dark heavens but could see nothing but a patch of clouds beginning to obscure the bright twinkling of stars and the whitish-blue glow of the full moon. Then Bao tripped in a rut, picked himself up and dusted his trousers with the flat of his hand. Without a word he walked back to his place at the camp fire, sat down and finished his meal.

FETTERMAN LEANED OUT the open door to look for landmarks that would indicate the drop zone. As he hung out into space, the prop wash set his shirt collar to fluttering while Gerber held him firmly by the web of the harness so he wouldn't fall out of the aircraft.

Fetterman searched the ground below for the reflection of the moon off the Red River and the highway. He gritted his teeth. Clouds obscured the sky, blocking the starlight. Overhead, Fetterman knew the moon was full, and if their luck had been right he would have been able to see five hundred feet below, where the jungle rivers and streams would have looked like molten lead in the moonlight. But on this jump, he would have to trust the Air Force's navigation skills.

Fetterman felt a sourness welling up in the pit of his stomach. Army airborne troops had been the victim of Air Force incompetence and even cowardice before. During World War II, the Air Force had dropped the Eighty-Second Airborne Division on the wrong drop zone during the invasion of Normandy. Weighed down by weapons and ammo, dozens of paratroopers died when they landed in flooded fields. And on another occasion cowardly pilots seeking to avoid ground fire dropped paratroopers too low for their canopies to open. Fetterman trusted this operation would be right on target.

Forward in the cockpit, the red glow of the instrument panel reflected eerily off the flight crew's faces as the navigator pointed through the windscreen at the place where he had calculated the drop zone would be. When he throttled back the engine, Bocker and the rest went through the routine by the numbers: stand up, hook up, sound-off for equipment check, check equipment, hook up their static lines and bunch up by the paratroop door.

Gerber and Fetterman had painstakingly interpreted the map and picked a good drop zone. The DZ, from what they were able to divine from the features detailed on the map, would not be dotted with boulders that could break a paratrooper's leg or ankle bones. Hopefully the only hazard they would encounter would be soiling their boots on slippery water buffalo dung.

The light flashed red over the door. "Get ready," shouted Gerber. Anxiously the men waited for the green light.

Dirty Shirt's stomach went wild with anxiety. He made a mental note to relax. Break no bones, he prayed.

Bocker looked at the Air Force loadmaster; he and Gerber were busy screaming into each other's ears over the roar of the engines. Bocker yanked one of the first-aid kits free from the bulkhead and tucked it under his arm. Fetterman saw the action and did the same.

The light went green and Gerber went out the door first. Fetterman, Kai and Krung followed in rapid succession.

Just as Bocker stepped up to the door, the Air Force guy spotted the red cross emblazoned across the front of the first-aid kit. Instantly Bocker leaped out into space. The loadmaster yelled frantically after him, "Hey, come back here with that . . ."

Hot prop wash blasted Bocker's face. The taste of oily exhaust hung thick on his tongue as his parachute deployed, then inflated. He looked around for the landmarks that would prove they had been let out over the drop zone, but the clouds were still obscuring the moon.

Silently, the team descended together with the sound of the aircraft disappearing into the night sky.

Almost to the ground, Bocker lowered his H-harness so that his rucksack hung a few feet below him and so that when he landed he wouldn't be tangled in it or drive it painfully between his legs.

8

THE DROP ZONE NEAR
PHU THO, NORTH
VIETNAM

After gathering up their parachutes and stuffing them in the aviation kit bags the men assembled around Gerber. "Any broken ankles?" he asked, peering into the assemblage of blackened faces.

"Krung's missing. Where's Krung?" asked Fetterman, looking around. Krung had been the second man out of the plane and should have been at the assembly point by now.

"He went down somewhere over there." Bocker swept his arm off to the right where there was nothing but darkness.

As if on cue, Krung took that moment to appear out of the shadows and limp up to the group. He dropped his bundled-up parachute at his feet and let out a sigh. *"Dai uy,"* he said, to Gerber breathlessly.

"You okay?" asked Fetterman. "Any broken bones, sprained ankles?"

Now the clouds had passed off to the east and the moon glow reflected off Krung's dark forehead. He

nodded. "Bad exit from airplane." He explained how
he had inadvertently twisted as he went out the door,
didn't fall away clean, and how the prop wash had caught
him, slamming him hard against the fuselage two or
three times before he could fall away from the plane. He
joked that he could have counted the rivets that held the
skin of the aircraft. Luckily for his nose and teeth, the
rucksack had taken the brunt of the impact.

"So how many rivets are there, Trung Si?" cackled a
delighted Kai.

"Oh, fuck," said Bocker. "The radio." He grabbed
Krung by the shoulders, spun him, unstrapped the
rucksack and opened the flap. Not wanting to use a
flashlight and possibly betray their presence, he tucked
his hand inside and felt around the edges of the radio.

"What's the verdict?" said Gerber anxiously.

"Hell, I dunno. We may be all right. Right off I can't
feel if there's anything cracked or broken. But you never
know about a circuit board or the resistors. It's bad
enough trying to keep them from shorting out in the
humidity. We'll know more when we try to make
commo. Right now I just can't be sure."

To the southeast, and beyond the horizon, the sky
flickered, almost turning the night into a blue-white day.
It looked as if the world was ending. A few moments later
the ground trembled beneath their feet. Everybody
froze, listening for the muffled whump-whumps in the
distance.

"Arc light," said Gerber quietly. "The B-52s are
working out their aggressions on the bad guys with five-
hundred-pound iron bombs. Go Air Force." Gerber
raised his wrist and unfastened the flap to read the luminous dial of his Rolex watch: 0100 hours. Then he directed them toward the tree line. "Come on, let's get off

the DZ in case any of the locals saw our plane and the little parachutes that trailed out its ass end.''

Some weeks before, the monsoon rains had stopped falling, so Gerber and his men could negotiate the terrain with relative ease; boot-sucking mud would otherwise have slowed their progress. Gerber, Fetterman, Bocker, Dirty Shirt, Krung and Kai walked the paddy dikes kicking up red dust. They knew it was red even though it was still night. All of the dirt in Vietnam was red; it was as if all traces of black dirt had been bleached white by the tropical sun, only to be soiled again by decades' worth of blood spilled by fallen Japanese, Chinese, French, Vietnamese and American soldiers.

They walked about ten meters apart, and because the team numbered only six men they didn't bother positioning flankers out to either side. Their fragmentation grenades and canteens were fastened with strips of green tape to hold them tight and quiet. And even though it was a little hotter and stuffier to do so, they wore their sleeves rolled down and unbuttoned. The cloth protected their skin from the thorns and sawtooth leaves, and another welcome benefit was that under fire the sleeves would reduce burns from falling mortar fragments.

They also wore olive drab head scarves. The Americans had pulled them over the scalp and knotted them behind the head while Kai and Krung wore them as sweatbands, with the tails hanging down on one side of the face.

Once they were out of the clearing and starting into the trees, Bocker padded up alongside Gerber. Mindful of noise discipline he said in a low voice, "I'm worried about the radio. I'd like to run a commo check with the

SFOB. Besides, if it's not working it's just extra weight slowing us down.''

Gerber nodded and used hand signals to deploy the men in a crude semblance of a perimeter defense. ''Set up the radio and give me the verdict,'' he told Bocker.

Krung tugged the quick release on his rucksack shoulder strap and slipped it to the ground without having to awkwardly struggle to get it off his back. He opened the flap and brought out the PRC-74 transceiver and its long wire antenna. Bocker rigged a quarter-wavelength jungle antenna and hoisted the wire up into a tree with a nylon cord similar to a parachute suspension cord. With the earphones on his head, he sat down and plugged in the leg key.

Bocker slowly turned the frequency adjusting dial, skimming past the babble of commercial shortwave broadcasts and the whine of the Teletype machines. For a few minutes he listened to the latest number-one hit on the American top forty, courtesy of BBC. And from Radio Peking, he heard an English language broadcast by a female commentator, detailing the loathsome exploits of the bloodthirsty imperialist American soldiers.

''Crazy bitch,'' muttered Bocker. ''Hell, I haven't shot any slopes all goddamn week.'' Satisfied that the radio could at least receive, Bocker told Gerber they might as well try a transmission. Gerber brought out the one-time message pad. He dictated and by red lens flashlight wrote down the clear text message above the secret phrase they had left with Blauveldt. Doing so gave him a third row of letters that he would transmit back to the SFOB. Armed with the secret phrase, Blauveldt could decipher their codes.

With the encrypted message in hand, Bocker held down the Morse code key for a scant second, causing the transmitter to whistle a long dash in his earphones. With one eye on the field strength meter, he quickly adjusted the antenna load in order to maximize the transmitter's output. He would be sending a blind transmission back to the SFOB and the operators would not respond to him immediately. The wisdom of that was that if the enemy heard his CW they would not link him to the SFers.

Bocker began his communication by sending a short identifying string of Q and Z signals, alerting the SFOB to his presence and the fact that he would be sending a message in a matter of seconds. He sent one more Q signal, and then keyed twenty groups of five letters each. The last group was nothing more than a string of Xs encoded to foil any NVA code breakers who might be listening in.

Now Bocker switched the radio's frequency up 1 megahertz and waited for the SFOB reply, and found himself wondering if the good guys in the South had even heard him calling. Until they answered, he had no way of knowing if the message had gotten through. Bocker sat in the darkness listening to the crackling static for ten minutes. He swore under his breath and flipped back to the transmit frequency. He repeated the procedure of Q and Z signals followed by the message and then back to the receive frequency for the SFOB's reply. Nothing. After another ten minutes of listening to static, he switched off the radio, turned to Gerber and whispered, "Captain, I hate being the bearer of ill tidings, but my military mind tells me we are waist deep in some pretty smelly shit."

GERBER LEANED BACK against a towering teak, closed his eyes and tried to rest. It was an exercise of futility. His sleep was plagued by dreams wherein countless legions of VC wouldn't stay dead when they were shot. With little variation these were the all-too-familiar dreams that had troubled his sleep ever since his first day in combat.

On this night he dreamed that he and Fetterman were backed up against a storm-swollen river, and Gerber was holding off a squad of suicide-bent NVA. Whenever one of his bullets struck an enemy soldier it was as if he was a *hashasheen* hopped up on dope.

The black-pajama-clad warriors just kept on coming, the bullets piercing their bodies without bursting spleens or exploding hearts. Exasperated, and with his weapon emptied into the human wave, he reached down to reload and could only find .30-caliber ammunition, chambered for an M-1 carbine, which was unfortunate since he was carrying an M-16. Even though the dream about the river and the bad ammo bothered him to a certain degree he was used to them, so he just let them play as if it was a Saturday night movie. Even in his sleep he knew it was just a dream.

With the breaking of dawn, the sun brightened the heart of the jungle, changing it from black to dark green. As Gerber became aware of his surroundings, he felt an unnatural weight resting between his legs. A shiver ran up and down his spine as he hoped he was wrong. Without moving his head, he glanced down. A slender green snake with a narrow head and large eyes lay coiled between his inner thighs, its head resting on his crotch.

Sometime during the night the cold-blooded snake had crawled on top of him to share the warmth of his body's heat. Gerber froze, instinctively knowing that if he moved even a single muscle, he'd be slipped into a shallow hole, Fetterman would throw a handful of soil on his face, and he'd be buried in an unmarked grave in

North Vietnam. Not a good career move, he thought to himself. With great patience, Gerber lay still, watching the rest of the camp come to life.

Across the camp he watched as Fetterman opened his eyes and instinctively reached for his grease gun. He peered down its bore to make sure nothing had lodged in it during the night. Then he broke it open and started wiping it with an oily rag.

A little farther into the undergrowth Krung sat with his back against a tree. He had unsheathed his knife and started stropping the already razor-sharp edge on his leather belt while he quietly hummed a nondescript Oriental tune.

Fetterman stretched, yawned, got up and rather noisily tromped toward some bushes and unbuttoned his fly.

Nearby, Kai took a long pull from his canteen, got up and walked over to join Fetterman. The Montagnard started a stream and the two of them stood side by side, urinating against the foliage.

Bocker fiddled with the radio, muttering something to himself that Gerber could almost but not quite make out. Then Bocker threw his hands up in disgust, sighed and walked over to Gerber and started talking. ''Damn radio, I'm not sure it will transmit. Must have been the— Jesus Christ!'' Bocker had seen the green snake coiled up on Gerber's lap. He stopped dead in his tracks and just stared at the reptile with disbelief.

At Bocker's utterance, the other men grabbed for their weapons, but Bocker motioned to them back. ''Snake,'' he said in a muted tone.

The creature hadn't moved.

Neither had Gerber. Without a trace of fear on his placid face, he sat with his back against the tree and waited.

Warily Fetterman approached with his machete drawn and held high over his head, ready to strike. The master sergeant swallowed as he considered the options. Wedged as it was on Gerber's lap, it was impossible to slash at the snake with his long blade without ruining Gerber's chance for a wife and kids. A bullet would make too much noise. And probably so would Gerber.

Fetterman retreated to join the others, who now stood in a knot next to Bocker, surveying the situation.

"Well?" said Fetterman, looking at Bocker.

Bocker shrugged.

"No problem," said Dirty Shirt. And as calmly as if he were reporting for monthly pay in the orderly room, he walked ten paces to Gerber's feet, and in one rapid motion reached down and grabbed the snake just behind its head. With his free hand he grabbed it by the tail, changed hands and then began to whirl it overhead like a rodeo cowboy's lariat. He swung it faster and faster in an ever widening arc. The only sound was the snake's hissing and the whirring its body made as it swung around and around. At one point a length of its tail caught momentarily in the vines overhead. Losing the rhythm of the swing the fangs of the dizzy but angry serpent came perilously close to sinking into Dirty Shirt's neck.

"Enough diddling around. Kill it," said Bocker.

Dirty Shirt cracked the snake's body like a bullwhip and the snake's brain exploded with the backlash.

Dirty Shirt dangled the limp reptile by its tail; the head lay in the dirt, blood trickling out of the mouth. Now obviously the center of attention, Dirty Shirt stood proudly, his right arm held high above his head, and a good foot and a half of snake still lay on the ground.

Gerber shakily got to his feet and stared at the dead serpent's lifeless eyes and its bloody, forked tongue dangling in the dirt. Already the skin was beginning to lose its luster in death.

"How did you know it wouldn't strike?" said Bocker.

"I make him an eight-footer," said Fetterman.

"Seven anyway," said Dirty Shirt.

"So how did you know he wouldn't strike and kill both of you with a basic load of snake venom?" repeated Bocker.

Dirty Shirt laid the toe of his boot against a fist-size lump located six inches down the snake's throat. "He ate recently. Only have to worry about hungry snakes up in the vines, waiting to drop down and fill their bellies." He had emphasized the word hungry. "Besides, this is a krait, they never bite after the sun's up. I've watched Okinawan kids torture them for hours outside of Naha. Dozens of times." He let go of the tail and the long snake plopped unceremoniously onto the jungle floor. "Well, almost never."

Bocker's face blushed red. "Idiot," he said, trying to control his anger. "Kraits are black with yellow bands. Is that snake black? No. It's fucking green. That's a green mamba. Not a krait. You know, the cobra family. That was an immensely stupid move."

Dirty Shirt stiffened and held his breath.

In a quiet tone Fetterman added, "Ever hear of the two-step? If he had sunk his fangs into your ass, you'd have taken about two steps and fallen flat onto your nose. Dead before you hit the ground."

Kai and Krung chuckled.

Gerber's voice was quiet. "Worked out okay in the end. Hindsight's not twenty-twenty, it's myopic as hell. Let's not be second-guessing Dirty Shirt. He still saved

my life. Thanks, Shirt.'' Gerber shook Dirty Shirt's
hand.

When they let go of each other's hands, Dirty Shirt
brought his foot down on the snake's head and ground
his heel against the skull—once, twice, three times.

Fetterman laughed, ''Since you know so much about
snakes, Dirty Shirt, maybe you can tell us if this is a boy
snake or a girl snake.''

''Huh?'' said Dirty Shirt, looking up.

Fetterman jabbed Krung good-naturedly in the ribs.
'''Cause if it's a boy snake, Krung has got to do his duty.
This is clearly a Communist infiltrator.''

''Very funny,'' said Krung with a grin devoid of
mirth. ''Very funny.''

Gerber gave orders to break camp. ''We've got miles
to go before we sleep. Let's get the rucks up on our backs
and *di di mau*.''

Krung rolled the snake onto its back with the toe of
his boot. He stared at its pale, scaled belly for a few moments, grunted, then whirled and walked toward his
rucksack.

THROUGHOUT HIS TWO TOURS in Vietnam and in the
innumerable officers' clubs and civilian gin joints scattered across Southeast Asia, Gerber had listened to
straight-leg infantrymen droning on and on about how
the Army Map Service's topographical maps outright
lied, or at the very least were incredibly inaccurate. It
had to be so, said the legs, how else would you explain
it when the terrain underfoot didn't match the map's
legend? It was an all-too-familiar story of incompetence. In his own mind Gerber knew the maps had never
been wrong. The truth was that the legs were lost and
weren't even bright enough to know it.

And now ironically Gerber was somewhere in North Vietnam, and the ridge lines and other features detailed on his map didn't agree with the terrain in front of him. That meant either the map was wrong and the legs had been right all along, or the Air Force had sloppily dropped Gerber's team somewhere other than the LZ they had designated. Gerber decided to trust the map and not the Air Force. And that meant they were lost in the jungle, and they could be almost anywhere in North Vietnam or even Laos.

Gerber brought the OD binoculars to his face and adjusted the focus as he thought out the problem. He muttered an oath as he scanned the valley before him. His anxiety was obvious to anyone looking at his clenched jaw, to anyone who had heard the inflection behind his blue language. He shook his head, realizing that it wasn't the way to handle the situation. He quelled his anxiety, not wanting the men to sense something might be horribly wrong.

"We lost?" asked Bocker, betting on his sixth sense.

Gerber shook his head. "No. But it is kind of like something that happened to Daniel Boone once."

"Huh . . . ?"

"When Daniel Boone was an old man, some wise-ass newspaperwoman from New York interviewing him asked, 'You with the reputation for being a hotshot woodsman and all, Daniel, were you ever hopelessly lost?' According to the story they tell on the orienteering course at Fort Benning, Boone thought about it for a while and answered that no, he hadn't ever been lost. Then he was quiet for a couple of minutes, letting that sink in. Finally, he went on to say that on occasion he'd been a mite bewildered for days on end. But he had never been lost. . . ."

Bocker immediately grasped the significance of their situation. "I get it. Like Boone, we're not lost, we're just a mite bewildered."

Gerber smiled and jabbed a finger at him. "Now you get the deal. Everything is under control." Gerber knew from years of experience that in situations like this, panic could be a bigger enemy than the enemy himself. He knew that at all costs he had to maintain control of the situation.

Fetterman pursed his lips and pointed in a vague direction off into the depths of the jungle. "No problem," he said cheerfully. "I know exactly where we are and what's ahead. East Bum Fuck Egypt, twenny miles this-a-way."

Gerber went back to his binoculars and continued to search the length and breadth of the valley. "I'm looking for landmarks, anything we can see that we can relate to the map. If I find anything that we can place on the map we can figure out where in the hell we are by a process of elimination." After about five minutes of studying the terrain, he put down the binoculars and grabbed the map. "Smokestack," he said. "Though I can't actually see it, I can see a wisp of smoke coming from it. That's just as good. Check the map, Sergeant Fetterman. Look for anything that might give off smoke."

Fetterman leaned over the map and studied the zig-zag lines and loops. With a dumbfounded expression he tapped the map twice with his index finger and looked up into Gerber's eyes. "Right here, Captain. Right here."

Gerber hunkered down next to him, studied the location he had pointed to and then nodded. "You're right, Tony. There it is." He took out his engineer's compass, allowed for the difference between true north and magnetic north and oriented the map so the longitude of the earth lined up with the longitude of the map. After a few moments' calculation he had the information he needed. "Way to go Air Force," he said with an undisguised tinge of sarcasm. "Only ten klicks off course."

Fetterman cursed, then went on to say, "It's my fault, I know better than to trust the Air Force. I couldn't see the DZ through the clouds. We should have aborted rather than take the chance. It's my fault."

Bocker whistled. "Ten klicks, huh? Looks like we're gonna be here for longer than we planned." He unzipped the Air Force first-aid kit, removed the amphetamine-laced candy bar and handed it to Gerber. "I believe we might all be developing a taste for candy in the next few hours."

Gerber unwrapped the foil package, broke off one of the chocolate squares and popped it into his mouth. He chewed it twice and then swallowed it. He passed the bar on to the next man. "So we're not lost anymore. But we are off course. It doesn't matter. It is true that this complicates things a little bit in the sense that we'll never be able to complete the mission according to schedule."

"Change forty-seven," said Fetterman wryly. He was referring to the fact that on a mission the best laid plans often failed and one needed to improvise, to go with the flow. Thinking on your feet and coping with changes was as necessary and vital as loading your weapon.

"Change forty-seven, and we'll probably change plan again and again and again. The Air Force blew it. There's no question. But we don't have to die for it. And there's no sense in scrapping the mission. So change forty-seven is that we'll be a day late getting to our target. So let's hat up and move out.''

SIX HOURS HAD DRAGGED by since they had walked away from the tree line adjacent to the drop zone. Gerber and his men had climbed hills, tangled themselves in vines, tripped, fallen flat on their faces and grown increasingly thirsty. To a man they found it ironic that in a tropical rain forest there was never enough drinking water. Not ever.

Some stretches of the trail they followed were clear enough to run down them full speed as if they were sidewalks flanking the wide boulevards in Saigon. Traversing the ten klicks would put them behind schedule but there was simply no way to move fast through the jungle. The only thing the survival rations would do was help them keep going beyond their normal level of endurance.

Fetterman found that most of the time he had to alternately lift his knees chest-high to be able to step over fallen tree trunks, and then sink down onto his haunches and duck-walk so his head could clear the grabbing of the overhead vines.

Worse than duck walking he hated the wait-a-minute vines that grew randomly across the steamy green tangle of jungle. It was almost as if the skinny vines were conscious of their presence, waiting like diabolical creatures to reach out and loop around an ankle.

An encounter with one left a man with two choices: Either wait a minute and shake the vine off your boot, or crash through like a bull. A man inexperienced in the ways of the jungle would mistakenly try to crash his way through the shrubbery. Inevitably the vines would see to it that he lost his footing. To break his fall, his natural reaction would be to grab the nearest tree, invariably a thorn tree. Its trunk was porcupined with long, black needles that jabbed deep into fingers and palms of the hands and then inconveniently broke off flush with the skin. Twenty-four hours later, the dozens of embedded slivers would have festered into an ugly infection that throbbed painfully. Months later the slivers would still be working their way out of his body.

Pausing a minute here and there as necessary, Fetterman climbed straight up and down the sides of mountains. The slopes were overgrown with trees, brambles, bushes, vines and slippery rocks. At one point he had estimated their progress was averaging no more than a measly one hundred meters per hour. Krung on point could have hacked a trail through the foliage with his machete to make the path easier going, but swinging the blade would have worn him out very quickly and left an easy-to-spot trail, thereby allowing the NVA to detect their presence and follow in their footsteps.

So they did it the hard way, climbing the sides of mountains and descending into the valleys on the other side. Some of the streambeds crisscrossing the trail were as dry as a sun-parched desert rock, while in other valleys flowed crystal-clear water with leaves of green floating lazily on the surface. And even though the water looked as pure and as inviting as the Rocky Mountains springs shown on the TV beer commercials, no one felt the temptation to cup a hand in the water and drink from it. Fetterman knew that to do so would have been to chance a gut-wrenching and incapacitating illness hundreds of miles behind enemy lines. Experience had taught him that the overgrown jungle was very good at defending itself from mere humans.

As Fetterman walked at the rear of the column, he looked at Gerber, Bocker, Dirty Shirt and then transferred his gaze to Krung and Kai. The master sergeant noticed some very obvious differences between Occidental and Oriental anatomy. He found himself wondering why Krung's and Kai's trousers hung high in the front and low in the back, while the overfed Americans' profile was just the opposite. Chalk it up to a rice and fish diet versus cheeseburgers and fries, he concluded.

They hadn't eaten for nearly twenty-four hours and yet he wasn't the least bit hungry. In the stifling heat and humidity his appetite had faded, but thirst had grown into a voracious beast until it gnawed away in the back of his mind as strongly as a heroin addiction. His most precious commodity was the water in his two-quart canteens stored in his rucksack. Forget measuring progress in distance per hour. More realistically it should be gallons per hour, he thought.

As they descended into a nameless valley, Kai stopped by the edge of a wide stream and placed his rifle butt on the ground. Soon the rest of the team caught up to him.

"We'll take a ten-minute water break," directed Gerber, who was breathing hard from the day's exertion. Besides giving them the breather they needed, taking a break would give him a chance to locate their position on the map and measure their progress.

The men pulled off their rucksacks and sank to the ground, resting with their backs against the sky-tall trees. They were coated from head to toe with jungle mud from their slipping and sliding on the trail. All around them wildly colored birds scolded their intrusion.

"Ssh," said Fetterman suddenly, cocking an ear skyward as he jumped to his feet. "Hear it? Anybody hear it?'' Wearily they all nodded, but no one appeared to possess the vigor Fetterman displayed.

"Probably American or North Vietnamese fighters," mumbled Gerber without emotion as he unrolled his map. He had sealed it in laminated plastic so the water wouldn't cause it to disintegrate in his fingers.

Fetterman shook his head and sat back down. He closed his eyes and continued to concentrate on what he could hear, knowing that an audible landmark was as useful as one you could see. Soon he was able to pick out the faraway whine of tires on a highway, the squeal of brakes, followed by silence, then the engine running back up through the gears. The vehicle sounded deceptively close, but from experience Fetterman knew that the highway traffic could easily be ten miles away.

Bocker sat on the stream bank, kneading his weary calf muscles and began to feel the dull ache disappear. All the while he massaged his leg, he considered the muddy water, which looked as if it could be forded easily. But he knew that might not be the case because current and depth could be deceiving. He reached into his rucksack and pulled out a canteen, shaking it to determine whether there was any water left in it. He called to the others, "I'm going to fill one of my canteens and dump in some purification tablets. Anybody else's is empty I'll do his, too."

Gerber sat cross-legged on the bank, his muddy pants stuck to his legs and the map spread on his lap. Feeling a strange tickling on the back of his hand, he looked down and saw that a leech had attached itself to him. A cold shiver ran up and down his spine; he would never grow accustomed to leeches. He despised the loathsome creatures and the way they lived. He knew leeches spent most of their lives patiently waiting on the floor of the forest and the leaves of bushes. When they sensed the vibration of a passing step they leaped across the forest floor and onto a passing mammal to secure a meal of blood.

Gerber's leech had already swollen to grotesque proportions. Calmly, Gerber stood up, pinched its tail hard between his thumb and forefinger. Reacting immediately to the pressure, the leech released itself and vomited a gout of blood onto Gerber's skin. Then it tumbled to the ground, and undaunted by the pinch or the fall, began to loop enthusiastically back toward his boot.

Gerber shook his head, "Wrong," he said, place-kicking the squirming creature into the water.

"This stream on the map, Captain?" asked Fetterman as he looked across to the other side. He found it ironic that a waterway detailed as a mere stream in Vietnam would constitute a respectable river back in the real world.

"Dunno. We're about to find out," replied Gerber, first unlacing and then slipping off his jungle boots. Barefooted, he carefully waded into the swift-moving water. As it eddied around his knees and then up to his waist, Gerber walked up and down the stream, looking as if he had lost something and was trying to find it.

"Find any rocks?" called Fetterman from the shore-line.

Gerber nodded, sloshing back to shore. "Yeah, there's enough rocks on the streambed for it to be here year round. I was afraid this might be runoff from a rainstorm upstream. But I couldn't find any grass when I wiggled my toes."

Fetterman knew that if it was only runoff it wouldn't be marked on the map. But since it was a bona fide stream it would be on the map, and therefore they had found another landmark.

"Boy, that water felt good," said Gerber. He didn't bother to wring out his fatigues, knowing that the heat would evaporate it in a short time.

When Gerber had first started into the water, Dirty Shirt had also pulled off his boots and his socks, but for a different reason. "Damn jungle rot," he mumbled with a scrunched-up face, savagely digging his fingernails into his own flesh. "Itches so bad I feel like pouring gasoline between my toes and torching it. Damn."

Fetterman nodded sympathetically. "Sooner or later you get jungle rot. And once you've got it, it never gets cured, it just goes dormant. Just like malaria waiting in the dark, biding its own sweet time for the worst possible moment to strike."

"Happiness is dry feet," said Kai, nodding sagely. "I never jungle rot my feet."

"How's that?" asked Dirty Shirt, slipping his socks back on.

"Secret remedy." Kai giggled. "Pee on feet never get rot."

Dirty Shirt thought for a moment. "I think I'd rather suffer through. That's just not something I could do." He wondered if Kai was telling the truth and wondered if the aggravation of his burning feet would ever get to be so bad that he'd really be tempted to at least try the proffered cure.

By then Bocker had gathered up all of their empty canteens and had waded into the swift-flowing stream, where he squatted and then dunked the collection of green plastic, two-quart bladders into the clear running water. The canteens blooped out big bubbles as liquid displaced air.

Fetterman hooked a thumb and pointed over his shoulder, "Kai and I are going to have a look upstream." Bocker nodded as the two of them started walking toward the north.

They walked along the riverbank in silence. Almost at once Fetterman's nose caught the unmistakable whiff of fish. A moment later Fetterman noticed blood-speckled fish entrails and a sprinkling of scales lying on the bank where they had fallen from the edge of the knife. He halted and pointed them out to Kai, but the Oriental had already seen them. It seemed obvious to Fetterman that someone had recently caught and cleaned a catch at the water's edge.

That in itself wasn't an unlikely occurrence; after all, they were in a populated area. But the discovery did dictate the need for caution. Now even more alert, they continued walking upstream, searching for other signs of human presence. Kai stayed on the bank while Fetterman hunkered down into a crouch. Slowly he padded up the stony creek bed with the ripples of water breaking around the ankles of his boots.

He moved upstream to where the water was mirror smooth and shone green from the reflection of overhanging branches. Fallen leaves bobbed on the surface. A black shadow darted in the water by his side, startling him for a moment. "Hey, there are fish here." Then he remembered they already knew that from the scales they had come across and he felt stupid. He asked Kai, "How do we catch one?"

Kai didn't answer. Instead he slung his rifle over his shoulder, waded knee-deep into the water and stood motionless in a wide-legged stance with hands poised ready above the surface. Spotting a fish working its way upstream, he held his breath and let it swim between his legs. When the moment was right, he reached in and grabbed a fat little fish out of the water.

Fetterman gaped in amazement. "Let's have a look," he said.

"I kill it first," said Kai, struggling to hold on to the wriggling creature.

"Don't let it slip out of your hands," advised Fetterman, but before he could finish the sentence, Kai had slapped its head against a rock, instantly killing it. Working quickly and confidently, he drew his knife from its sheath, cut its head off and slit open its belly.

Out of the corner of his eye Fetterman saw a huddled shape by the edge of the water. Startled, he whirled with his grease gun leveled in the firing position. After a moment he lowered the barrel of the weapon and let out a low, barely audible whistle.

Bocker jerked his head at Fetterman's signal and looked in the same direction; the bubbles had almost stopped breaking the surface of the water as the team's submerged canteens were nearly filled. He waded to shore, threw the canteens on the bank, grabbed his rifle and joined Fetterman.

Fetterman solemnly pointed to the ground. A few meters from his feet, a man lay facedown in the clear running stream.

"Shit," said Bocker, scowling. He was upset because he would have to upend the canteens and pour out the contaminated water. The thought of drinking corpse-befouled water raised bile in his stomach.

Fetterman worked his way along the muddy bank until he stood directly over the body. It was an old man, as his scraggly white beard and deeply furrowed face indicated. The fingers were clenched around a bamboo fishing pole that had shattered into pieces when he had collapsed on top of it.

"He looks a bit like Ho Chi Minh," said Fetterman, with a laugh.

By now Bocker stood right beside him. "He's dead, right?"

Fetterman knelt beside the corpse and touched its face. "Cold as a whore's heart. Yeah, he's dead. Give me a hand."

Bocker squatted next to him.

"Sorry about bothering your eternal slumber, old man." With great reverence, Fetterman grabbed hold of one shoulder and flipped the dead man over onto his back.

Suddenly the whiff of fish in the air was stronger.

"There," said Fetterman, pointing to the flattened wad of banana leaves that had been lying under the man's chest.

Bocker unwrapped the leaves and found a fillet of white meat.

"Found the scales and entrails downstream," said Fetterman.

Both men noticed that the part of the corpse that had been closest to the ground was mottled a deep purple. The blood had settled within a few hours of his heart's stopping. A sure sign of death.

"Natural causes?" said Bocker.

"Your guess is as good as mine." Fetterman shrugged. "I don't see any bruises or other signs of bloodletting. The old guy's heart probably hung up for a beat or two and he dropped in his tracks."

The two men got to their feet, stepped back and studied the body. Neither one said a word for a few minutes while they considered the situation.

"We'll leave him as we found him," said Fetterman. "Come on, help me turn him over onto his back."

Bocker nodded. "Somebody'll come looking for him and find him."

Fetterman pointed upstream past the body. "Come on. Let's get that water we were after."

Kai shook his head. "Too bad for him," he muttered. "Bad mistake for anyone to die away from home."

Fetterman was poised to ask Kai if he was superstitious about death and dying but decided against it when he remembered the night in the team house when they had drunk all that whiskey and talked about the ghost army of Vietnam.

He already had his answer.

While Bocker had been filling the canteens, Gerber had been studying the map. "We need to cross here," he told his men. "It's too wide to wade so we'll ford here with Australian poncho rafts."

Bocker gave Dirty Shirt a good-natured jab to the shoulder. "Hey, Shirt, you're not HALO qualified, what I want to know is, can you swim?"

"Come out in the deep water with me and find out," countered Shirt.

The men paired off and went to work on the river crossing. Bocker spread his poncho flat on the ground and he and Shirt laid both of their rucksacks on top of it with a rifle on either side. They rolled it up tightly so that it looked like a big green sausage, and then wrapped the entire bundle in Dirty Shirt's poncho. Finally, Dirty Shirt tied both ends with suspension cord. It took less than five minutes for the men to rig the rafts.

"If everybody's ready let's not be afraid to get our feet wet," said Gerber. "Assembly point is one hundred meters downstream and on the other side. Let's do it."

Bocker and Dirty Shirt were the first pair of men into the water. Together they waded into the stream, holding their poncho raft in front of them like a log. With water up to their chins, they hung on and started kicking against the current, working their way across to the opposite shore.

"Ouch," shrieked Dirty Shirt. "Something just bit me in the ass. Jesus, I think I'm bleeding."

"Well, don't worry." Bocker laughed. "It's dead now, whatever it is."

9

NVA AIR BASE NEAR PHU THO, NORTH VIETNAM

Fetterman made the observation that from the very first step into the wilderness, man and his rucksack and rifles stood out as boldly as if they had been painted with the brightest of fluorescent orange colors. But after spending two days in the jungle, he and the others had started to blend in with their surroundings.

The pigment of their skin and the fabric of their garments and webgear had been dirtied and dampened to the extent that they no longer gleamed as brightly as a Tu Do Street neon light. Instead, Fetterman's face and the back of his hands were grimy and brown. His fatigues, wrinkled and without shape, provided him with a natural camouflage that erased man-made geometric patterns and replaced them with nature's own colors.

He felt as if the benevolent jungle had embraced him within the shadows of giant palm and fern plants in order to protect him from harm. With infinite wisdom, Nature had subtly camouflaged him a little at a time with his gentle breathing. Even the mosquitoes and other carnivorous bugs had stopped biting. Perhaps that was because the sickly, sweet fragrance of soap and showers had been steamed from his armpits by sour sweat. But for whatever the reason, the formerly merciless mosquitoes no longer seemed interested in drawing Fetterman's blood in an unfair exchange of microscopic malaria parasites.

Fetterman lay hidden in the undergrowth on the top of the hill, with his binoculars against his eyes, scanning the wide bend of the Red River Valley barely a klick away. He noticed its muddy banks were tangled with foliage that crept right down to the water's edge. Then he swept the lenses shoreward and studied the military fortifications at Phu Tho.

Incredibly, there were no guard towers, no perimeter wire and no killing fields. Then he recalled that this was North Vietnam, and there was no reason for those things. In the strictest sense of the word, all of South Vietnam was the front lines and all North Vietnam was behind the lines. So the North Vietnamese military had seen fit to cut back the bush and jungle only minimally, and there was no open ground. It would also be extremely unlikely that the teams would find any booby traps or land mines; nonetheless, they would remain alert to that possibility as they infiltrated the camp.

Fetterman counted a dozen buildings that were obviously barracks, long and low buildings with corrugated tin roofs and rows of small windows.

At one end of the camp was a shedlike structure and a big red fuel tank supported by four legs, its filler hose drooping down to the dirt where a careless soul had simply let it fall after filling up a vehicle. A hundred meters to the east and down a narrow blacktop road was a low, squat building made out of cement blocks. Behind this two-story building with steps leading up to it rose a tall antenna supported by a maze of guy wires.

Fetterman looked closer and could see black coaxial cable strung from inside the building out to the antenna. In front of the building was a flagpole flying the blue, red and yellow flag of the NLF. Probably the headquarters and where the radio transmitter was located, he figured.

Fetterman watched as two men exited the headquarters building and walked toward the barracks. One of them wore the khaki-green uniform of an NVA officer, the other wore the khaki of a Chinese officer. Through the lenses, he could see their lips move, but from the great distance couldn't hear the words as the two officers bantered in animated conversation. Fetterman scanned the camp for other Chinese soldiers but didn't see any. When he swung the glasses back around to focus on the two officers they had already disappeared into one of the buildings.

Behind the HQ building was the airstrip. From the briefing reports he had read during the isolation phase of the mission, Fetterman recalled how the airstrip had originally been an ill-fated French installation more than a decade ago. For years after the French defeat at Dien Bien Phu, grass and weeds had grown up between the cracks in the slabs of the abandoned concrete runway. That had changed with the escalation in the war with the United States. Now the airfield was a landing site for Russian cargo planes ferrying in war matériel. He could see the physical evidence to that fact; off to one side of the taxiway, crates of ammunition and drums of aviation gasoline were piled high. A hundred meters away from the temporary ammo depot, two shiny Russian tanks were berthed.

Gerber crawled out of the trees to huddle next to Fetterman. Motioning toward the air base, he handed the field glasses to Gerber. "Look to the right of the taxiway, about a hundred meters," he directed.

Gerber took the binoculars. "Hmm, Russian tanks."

"Yeah, the tanks." Fetterman paused for a moment until the captain removed the field glasses from his eyes. "So what do you think?"

Gerber handed back the binoculars and the two men exchanged glances. They had spent enough time together that each one already knew what the other thought. Under normal circumstances Gerber considered it prudent to avoid contact whenever deployed behind enemy lines. It was common sense, he figured, when you were outnumbered by only about a million to one to keep your nose clean. But there were always exceptional situations. Gerber shrugged. "As long as we're here. Why not? Once we've accomplished our primary mission and planted the tulips we'll give the enemy troops a live-fire training opportunity."

"It's the least we can do for their war effort," said Fetterman. "But then what? You figuring on escaping and evading to the coast?"

Once again Fetterman lifted the glasses to study the target further.

"We both know it's a long shot," said Gerber. "But we don't have any other choice as I see it. Since we can't communicate with Nha Trang, they don't know where or when to send our helicopter. Another day or two and we'll be listed as missing in action. Just another one of the spike teams that mysteriously disappeared from the face of the earth."

Conversation lapsed as Gerber shrugged off his rucksack, feeling the heady relief that only comes after you've lost twenty pounds of dead weight from your shoulders that you've been carrying all day. He tapped the side of his ruck and said, "I'll be glad to get rid of these SIDs and claymores. No matter what the outcome, at least we'll be traveling lighter after tonight."

Fetterman looked at the HQ building and the antenna, envisioning how they might organize the assault. His face lit up suddenly. "Wait a minute," he said, lowering the binoculars. "We can talk to Nha Trang." Fetterman remembered having read about the installation when he was in isolation. He recalled that the transmitter put out somewhere around a thousand watts. More than enough to get through to the SFOB. "Hey, Captain. Why not capture the transmitter intact and use it to contact the SFOB?"

Gerber was stunned by the simplicity of the suggestion. "Of course," he agreed, understanding the plan. "If we can raise Group on the radio, then we could exfiltrate by helicopter rather than E and Eing our way to the coast."

"Why didn't I think of it before now?" said Fetterman, beginning to grin evilly. "And there's another possibility we haven't considered. The code books."

Gerber furrowed his brow. "Sure we can do it, no problem. But let me play devil's advocate for a moment. Why even bother to screw with them, even if we exfiltrate in a timely manner and get the code books back most ricky-tick, what have we gained? A day or two at most before their net control figures they've missed too many scheduled communications, and they send out a platoon of grunts and find out they've been compromised."

"And find out they're minus a transmitter site," corrected Fetterman with a twinkle in his eye. "Oh, they'll be royally pissed off. You can count on it."

Gerber pressed on. "Okay. So we won't end the war by Christmas by stealing the code books, and Bob Hope will be on the road to Saigon one more time. On the other hand, if we do snatch the code books I guarantee we'll screw up their operations. Assuming this station is one of those that transmits instructions to the NVA regulars in the South, grabbing their codes and ciphers leaves them with two choices. Quit communicating until they can rush new code books to the South via the Ho Chi Minh Trail, and that'll take weeks. Or they can send their messages in the clear until they restore integrity to their crypto system."

"They'll be in a world of hurt no matter what they do," added Fetterman. "Either way their commo is compromised."

"I like it. I like it real well," said Gerber.

Fetterman nodded. "I guess it doesn't take a military mind to figure out we're going to knock 'em off the air and steal their secrets."

They killed time and passed the heat of the afternoon lying quietly in the shade, taking turns watching the camp over the remaining hours of daylight. Even though they weren't exerting themselves, they sweated heavily.

When it had been dark for more than an hour Gerber briefed them on the mission's objectives and how they were going to go about it. "And the only prisoner we take alive is the radio transmitter," he cautioned. "Remember we need the radio to get out of here. Otherwise it's a long, hard walk to the Gulf of Tonkin." Then he directed them to move out. Fetterman and Kai went off in one direction, Gerber and the others took off in another.

Moving slowly and listening to the sounds of the jungle, Fetterman and Kai worked their way down the gentle slope of the hillside. Although it was dark, the two of them were very careful to take maximum advantage of the cover provided by the foliage, dodging from tree to tree and bush to bush. When one man moved, the other stood by with his weapon held at the ready. Fetterman could have done it with his eyes closed, he had done it this way countless times before.

He led the way, stepping carefully, rolling his feet from heel to toe so he wouldn't inadvertently snap a twig or rustle the decaying vegetation. He froze as a gust of wind carried a faint whiff of diesel fuel to his nostrils. That meant they were very near to the tree line. He sank to his haunches and signaled Kai down.

The two men had drawn the job of planting the tulips. And now the Special Forces sergeant was only a few meters away from the location Major Blauveldt had specified. From his hiding place in the bushes, he looked down the road that led to the Phu Tho air base and supply depot. Fetterman shifted his gaze to the other direction where the road led to the west, making a wide bend and then pointing southwest toward the Laotian border and the upper reaches of the Ho Chi Minh Trail.

A half mile past the bend in the road and on either side in the ditches was where Blauveldt had told them to plant the seismic intrusion devices. It was a good location, Fetterman thought, *if* the electronic devices detected troops on the move and not monsoon rains beating the earth, trees swaying in the wind or an elderly mama-san riding a bicycle to market.

The two men broke out of the tree line and walked down the side of the road. "Here. This is the spot," said Fetterman. Then they divided the tulips between themselves and began to plant a row of them on opposite sides of the road.

Down on both knees, Fetterman scooped a shallow hole in the earth with his knife, shoved a SID into it and hastily covered it. It reminded him of laying a field of antipersonnel mines, like the diminutive Model 25 that would punch a hole through a soldier's boot and foot. Then Fetterman noticed that the mound of earth heaped over the SID looked unnatural and was sure to be spotted. The solution was simple, he brushed some of the excess soil away so that the ground was level. He was about to tamp it firm with the sole of his boot, but thought better of it, not wanting to chance injuring the delicate electronic gear and instead went on to planting the next device.

Installing all of the SIDs took only a few minutes. Somehow it seemed anticlimactic of Fetterman, to fly for hours in an airplane, rush pell-mell through the jungle to their destination; and days' worth of planning and physical exertion culminated in five minutes elapsed time.

Fetterman heaped earth over the last SID. "Hey, Kai," he whispered. "You think these fancy gizmos are sensitive enough to pick up the dead French paratroopers when they're wandering up and down these roads."

By now Kai was finished and he walked to Fetterman's side of the road. "You joke me, Sergeant Tony. Real funny. But if I get kill, I visit Song Be. Bring ghost soldier to your hootch. Scare you beaucoup. You see." For a moment Fetterman was worried that he had inadvertently offended the man with his attempt at humor, but under the glow of the moonlit sky Fetterman could see a smile beginning to break across Kai's face. "Maybe I not die, Sergeant Tony. Maybe you die, you join ghost army."

Fetterman got to his feet and brushed the dirt off his hands. "I don't think Mrs. Fetterman and the kids would appreciate that very much," he responded. "Besides, neither of us is going to get killed, Kai. Think of this mission like we're on a recruiting drive with the intent to get beaucoup Communists to die for Uncle Ho. We don't care how big their ghost army is. In fact the more NVA numbering the ranks, the merrier."

Mission accomplished, they headed off to rendezvous with Gerber and the others.

10

NVA AIR BASE PHU THO
NORTH VIETNAM

The night sky over North Vietnam was encrusted with stars and the soldiers on watch at Phu Tho airfield were as happy as a Montagnard tribesman with a handful of betel nuts to chew on. Their contentment was partly due to the fact that at Phu Tho there were no troublesome enemy soldiers to contend with. Located many miles to the west of Hanoi as they were, they could often see the flash of the bombs detonating on the horizon and feel the earth tremble underfoot, but they never had to scramble for cover, never had to bury a friend.

Yet even though the real shooting and dying of infantrymen occurred in South Vietnam, no soldier shirked his duty by catnapping on watch. Regardless of race, creed or politics, that was the ancient rule of warfare handed down from generation to generation. Too many honorable ancestors had learned the lesson too late to have done them any good. The unfortunate ones had thought of themselves as immortal. Death had enlightened their consciousness.

Huan patrolled the dim corners of the ammo dump. When the twenty-year-old conscriptee had come on duty, his pace had been quicker, but now he was beginning to tire. He found that walking the same path twenty times in an hour was about as exciting as leading a docile ox across a rice paddy. Over the innumerable months that he had been assigned to the air base ammo dump, his tired eyes had searched the darkness for faces that never appeared. He groaned in exasperation. Four in the morning was absolutely the worst time for anyone to draw guard mount. By the time he got off duty it would be too late to go back to sleep. The only thing he had to look forward to was breakfast in a few hours, followed by a long day of military drill and political lectures broken up by heavy lifting.

Hidden in the shadows a dozen yards away from the sentries, the Green Berets moved into position. With faces blackened and boonie hats pulled low over their eyes, Bocker and Gerber crouched at the edge of the jungle and watched Huan and the other slow-moving guards.

"This will be easy," whispered Bocker, unsheathing his commando knife. The long, thin blade was honed sharper than his grandfather's straight razor.

Behind the two men the brush rustled suddenly.

Bocker kept absolutely still.

Gerber's trigger finger stiffened instinctively.

"It's me," whispered Dirty Shirt, as he crouched down between his two partners.

"What did you see?" asked Gerber, in a muted voice.

"Tanks. Two of them. Alongside the hangars. Looks like the ammo for the main guns is loaded in trucks parked next to them."

Bocker smiled. "Still want to take them out?"

Gerber nodded. "Take Krung and Kai with you. I'm going to set out some claymore mines. Shirt, provide covering fire until we get back."

Moving along the edge of the compound Bocker watched for trip wires, depressions in the ground and weeds tied back, all indications of booby traps or mines. As he walked around the periphery of the generator shed and fuel tanks, he smelled the distinct odor of diesel oil, and noted darkened stains on the hard-packed ground.

Bocker followed the edge of the jungle until he could plainly see a tank silhouette, its cannon barrel pointed toward the horizon. He counted three men guarding the tanks. Using hand signals, Bocker assigned a guard each to Krung and Kai, saving one sentry for himself.

Bocker watched his man for a few moments before making his move. The guard was slow, and obviously tired of tramping around a cold hunk of steel in the middle of the night. He was probably preoccupied with thoughts about being in the arms of a favorite woman.

The American worked his way silently through the jungle until he was directly behind his target and then he padded slowly out of the trees. Patiently, he closed the distance, taking one step at a time, controlling each breath and forcing himself to remain calm. It wouldn't do to rush things. As Bocker crept toward his prey, his pulse beat faster as a fresh burst of adrenaline surged into his veins. He took two more steps and then he was standing directly behind the sentry.

Bocker stiffened and held his breath as he rocked back onto the balls of his feet. Ready to spring, he slowly pulled his Kabar knife from its leather sheath. His eyes shifted from side to side as he watched his target. He took the final step, and reached around the man's head to cup his big hand over the unsuspecting sentry's mouth. His

knife paused in midair and then he slammed the blade
into the sentry's kidneys. The steel went in easily.
Through the hand that muffled the scream Bocker could
feel saliva, and the quivering of wet lips. Against his
other hand he felt the warm gush of the blood. With all
of his strength, Bocker held the trembling sentry tightly
against his own body until the sentry's knees weak-
ened. Then he eased the dead guard to the ground,
withdrew the blade and wiped the blood on the enemy's
shirtsleeve. Then he peered around the corner of the
tank.

Krung and Kai waved. They had successfully eliminated their sentries as well.

Without a sound the Special Forces sergeant scaled the
tank hull. He recognized it as a PT-76, an amphibian,
and the same model that the NVA had used to overrun
the Special Forces camp at Lang Vei earlier in the
month. Bocker calculated the weight of explosive charge
necessary to cut through the steel armor plate, made a
generous allowance and then added a little more for good
measure. He had learned at the Demo Circle back at
Fort Bragg that it was better to set too large an explosive
charge than not enough. Besides, he didn't consider it a
reasonable endeavor to risk his life rigging a target light
for the sake of saving a few pounds of C-4 plastic explosives.

Bocker picked a spot where the turret mated with the
hull of the PT-76. Detonated at that precise location, the
flash of hot gases would slash through the steel and destroy the gear that rotated the turret. The shaped charge
would not devastate the tank, and the gun would still be
able to fire, but the damage to the gunworks would prevent the turret from rotating, rendering it a virtual eu-
nuch. Let them field a mobile gun emplacement with a

very limited field of fire, thought Bocker. It would be practically useless.

Once the formaldehyde-smelling plastic explosive was pressed into place, Bocker inserted the detonator into the lump of C-4. Next, he unshunted the electric detonator, connected the pair of wires to the timing device and set the delay. Finished with the first tank, he noiselessly slid down its side and padded over to the other PT-76 to wire it in a similar manner. Bocker performed like a master of black arts, operating on autopilot, blending explosives and steel. Satisfied with his work, he padded his way back to the tree line.

He took his place next to Gerber. Lying flat on his belly with the knife in his belt, he whispered, "All set." He unfastened the flap that covered his watch, and glanced at the luminous dial. "'Bout three minutes to go." Bocker's voice was trembling in anticipation.

Without a word, the men dispersed from their vantage point near the PT-76s, and took up new positions, aiming their weapons at the low wooden buildings that housed the off-duty guards.

The silence of the night was barely disturbed by two flat bangs that rang the tank hulls like a church bell.

Bocker figured the noise wasn't even loud enough to awaken the men in the barracks. Any of the light sleepers who had come to would groggily assume the sound to be nothing more serious than Hanoi taking a pounding from the B-52s, and would drift back off to sleep. But that didn't stop him from wondering whether or not the cutting charge had been sufficient enough to disable the tank.

Gerber stared at Bocker with a look that inquired whether or not he had fucked up the demolition. Then he followed up with the whispered question, "You sure you used enough explosives? Please reassure me we're not going to be chased into the jungle by two angry-as-mad-hornet tanks."

Bocker looked hurt. "Don't worry. I'm a man of finesse. I used just enough to do the job. And no more." He thumped his chest. "I'm a professional. Jeez. You're going to hurt my feelings."

"Right. Okay. Let's get on with it." Gerber sighted his AK-47 on the outside wall of one of the barracks and started firing, one shot at a time, working the bullets at an even interval.

The rattle of gunfire roused the sleepers and soon half-naked NVA soldiers spilled out of the barracks with AK-47s in one hand and their ubiquitous three pocket bandoliers of ammo in the other. Bent forward like men walking in heavy rain, they advanced toward the tree line where Gerber hid. The unsuspecting soldiers ran directly into the Green Berets' fusillade.

Gerber fired his automatic rifle in four-shot bursts, killing a handful of men. He noticed Krung and Kai were getting good kills. He smiled. He had painstakingly coached them, had told them that in a nighttime firefight, a man's natural tendency is to rise up over the rifle sights to see better. Gerber had taught the Yards to resist that temptation and make every round count. He had seen entire ARVN companies wiped out because the undisciplined troops had run out of ammo in the middle of a firefight. Gerber would never let that happen to his men.

"Now," shouted Gerber. On cue, Shirt offset the safety bail and depressed the handle on the electric firing device, detonating a string of claymore mines. The barrage of steel balls cut into the men, harvesting them like a reaper scything his way through a field of wheat.

Gerber had planted the claymores directly in front of a collection of fuel drums and the back blast split them open and ignited the contents.

Burst fifty-five gallon drums pinwheeled through the air; fingers of flames soared skyward. The fire spread until a cavalcade of explosions ripped through the nearby stacks of ammo. The flames burned a dirty yellow, and black oily smoke rose sky-high, then died for a moment before mounting suddenly again with a fresh explosion. One by one, mortar rounds still ensconced in protective cardboard tubes cooked off. The explosions vibrated the ground under Bocker, knocked the wind out of him. He lowered his rifle, shook his head and then wiped his index finger against the inside of his earlobe. He rubbed it against his thumb, feeling for the telltale trickle of blood that would tell him his eardrums had been burst.

One enemy soldier stunned by the concussion of a blast sat down hard. Seemingly oblivious to the clatter of gunfire, he just sat there with his torn scalp hanging down over an empty eye socket. He held his one good hand against the side of his face, trying to stanch the torrent of blood that washed relentlessly over his fingers.

Bocker ignored the ringing in his ears and started firing again, picking off the handful of men who were still standing. Taking careful aim on a man running for cover, Gerber squeezed the trigger and watched the man drop to the ground.

None of the enemy was left standing. The Green Berets ceased fire and the slight breeze cleared the battlefield of the last remnants of smoke. Cautiously Gerber and the others left the trees and starting walking toward the headquarters building and its radio room.

Gerber kicked open the front door and stepped in. The first floor was a single open room divided into bays filled with desks and filing cabinets. At the far end of the room he could see the radio and a maze of wires connected to it. A solitary NVA soldier, armed with an SKS carbine and looking like a scared filing clerk, blocked Gerber's way.

Gerber never hesitated. His AK popped twice, drilling the NVA with a bone-crunching shock. The clerk looked stunned as the impact hurled him backward onto the wooden floor.

Fetterman ran into the building and provided cover as Gerber whirled to his left and started up the flight of stairs. Fetterman followed. At the top they found a hall with doorways running along the walls on both sides. They checked each room, one at a time. At the end of the hallway there was one door left. Fetterman touched the knob. The door was locked. With his boot poised to deliver a kick, he yanked the pin on a grenade. A female voice screamed hysterically inside the room. "Don't shoot. Don't shoot." Fetterman hopped from one foot to the other, looking at the live grenade in his hand.

With his back against the wall, Fetterman yelled, "Come out with your hands in the air!"

From inside the room they heard footsteps running toward them. They pressed their backs against the wall as the door was flung open and suddenly they were staring at a blond woman. Gerber grabbed the wild-eyed woman by the arm and pulled her off to one side and slammed her hard against the wall.

Now they could hear another voice calling from inside the room, this time a man's voice. "I surrender. Do not shoot."

Fetterman still held the armed grenade in his grip. "Then come out and surrender." The voice had sounded too cool, too calculating. He was taking no chances.

"I am wounded. Come help me," came the feeble reply.

Fetterman looked to Gerber. "I don't trust him," he whispered.

"Me neither. You know what to do."

Fetterman nodded. "Okay. Here I come." With his back still against the wall he threw an empty M-3 magazine against the doorjamb where it clattered noisily then fell to the floor.

A hail of bullets cut through the door where Fetterman would have been standing. Fetterman relaxed his thumb and the spring-loaded arming spoon flipped away from the grenade. He counted aloud, "Five, four, three." Fetterman hurled the grenade into the open doorway, kicked it shut and then pressed his back against the stone wall. "Two, one."

The grenade detonated, knocking the door off its hinges. A cloud of dust billowed out of the room.

M-3 in hand, Fetterman reached his arm around the doorframe and fired a series of three-shot bursts into the room. Knowing anyone hiding in there who had survived the blast would be on his knees, he aimed low, raking the interior. The big, full metal jacket slugs ricocheted off the wall, making a horrible noise.

Fetterman stopped firing and waited for the dust to settle. His pulse was beating so hard he swore the sound would carry a mile. When he thought the time was right, Fetterman stepped into the room.

One of his bullets had caught the man in the face and had knocked off the back of his head. He was slumped over in his chair behind the desk. After he had been hit, his heart had continued to pump. Fetterman sidestepped the puddle of blood to avoid slipping in it, and walked right up to the body. "Scheming bastard," he said, kicking the chair and toppling him onto the floor.

Fetterman guessed his height to be about five feet ten inches, a good deal taller than the normal height of a North Vietnamese. Fetterman also noticed that instead of the expected NVA uniform he was wearing an unfamiliar khaki uniform. Fetterman stripped the brown leather belt from the belt loops and eyed the raised star embossed on the brass buckle. "Chinese," he intoned to himself, with a smile.

Fetterman stood over the body, studying the Oriental's face. He remembered his first tour of duty in Vietnam when they had run into a certain Chinese officer who had caused Special Forces in general, and Gerber and his detachment in particular, countless problems. They kept running across units he had trained that were trying to push the Green Berets out of Camp A-555.

After they went into Cambodia to assassinate him, they were indicted for murdering a foreign national in a neutral country. All this in spite of the fact that they had been ordered to make the hit. Fetterman remembered how he had thought he had killed the Chinese guy once in Cambodia, and another time in Hong Kong, and both times he had seemingly sprung back to life.

Looking at the dead man, Fetterman felt a flurry of contradictory emotions. In some ways he wished it was that same Chinese guy lying there in a pool of his own blood. And he also hoped it wasn't, because if it was, his death had come too quick and painless. In the end, the sergeant was sure that the Oriental in front of him was not their Chinese guy. Fetterman also trusted that someday their paths would meet.

11

**NVA AIR BASE PHU THO
NORTH VIETNAM**

The battle for Phu Tho was over. The blond woman who had surrendered to them inside the headquarters building sat in the radio operator's chair and sipped cool water from Gerber's polypropylene canteen.

"Thank you," she said. "I don't know why I'm so thirsty." She took deep gulps of the water as if she were drinking from a bottomless well.

She's never been really thirsty, thought Gerber. She's never had to wonder where her next bite of food or drink of water is going to come from, he surmised, pegging her as the kind of woman whose idea of a good time was shopping for the latest fashions. He decided that he didn't like her much.

"Who are you?" he asked gruffly. "And why are you here?" She was well-built, but a bit thin for Gerber's taste. With her green eyes and full lips, he couldn't help imagining what her baby-fine blond hair would look like when it became matted with sweat and clung to her brow.

"My name is Jane and I won't tell you my last name, I'm not very fond of giving it out to baby killers." She wiped her hand across her mouth and gave Fetterman back his canteen. "And I have a perfect right to be here. I've brought medicine and medical supplies to the Vietnamese people on behalf of my political party, the Alliance for Peace and Freedom."

Gerber's jaw dropped, and then he responded to her angry diatribe. "You're an American citizen and you brought medicine to the enemy? You're nothing more than a traitor."

"These people are not the enemy, they're needy souls," she countered. "I'm a pacifist. I don't believe in war. I just delivered a care package. That's all."

"She's lying," said Fetterman, controlling his temper. "She'd need an export license from the State Department. Not likely they would issue one to a traitor. With that blond hair she could be a Russian." He looked directly at her. *"Da tovarich!"*

By now Gerber's face had reddened, the veins stuck out in his neck, his fists were clenched. Fetterman noted that he had never seen the Green Beret captain this furious before.

"My, but you certainly seem stirred up," Jane told him in a huffy voice. "And you're right, the Philadelphia office applied for all the proper permits, but the paperwork was refused. So we circumvented all the red tape and shipped the goods to Japan and set sail from there without it. Our sailboat is at anchor right now in Haiphong harbor."

"Uh-huh," said Fetterman. "Maybe the last part of your story is true. But if it is, what are you, the self-avowed pacifist, doing on an NVA military installation?"

Gerber had regained his composure. "Let me see your passport...." He held out his hand.

She stared at it for a moment and then began to rummage through her backpack. When she found it she slapped it down into his hand. "Back at college we don't see the North Vietnamese as the enemy, we see them as human beings," she said. "We're more interested in peace and human brotherhood than war. Carrying supplies to suffering people can't be illegal in a decent society. But great gods of war that you are, you wouldn't understand that, would you?"

"Peace. Free love. Rah-rah-rah," said Fetterman, unimpressed.

"You never answered the question," said Gerber. "What are you doing on an NVA military base?"

She was silent for a moment and then answered, "I wanted to deliver the medicine in person. I had made a commitment to do so. I honor my commitments." She had stressed the word *my*. "A lot of people back home are counting on me to deliver it where it's needed worst."

Fetterman put his hands on his hips. "You know what, smart lady? Lenin called your type useful idiots. You're being used and you're too stupid to even know it."

Fetterman turned his back on her and asked Gerber, "So what are we going to do with Jane pinko?"

Gerber shrugged. "The way I see it, we have no choice in the matter. She's in the way. We don't have time to interrogate her to determine whether or not she's lying. We can't bring her with us because she would slow us down, and we can't really leave her or she can tip off the enemy." He paused for a moment to let the seriousness of her plight sink in.

"She *is* an American citizen," said Fetterman in a hushed tone.

"I understand that. Got any suggestions as to how we might spare her life?"

"Sure. We leave her and somehow incapacitate her so she can't get us killed by opening up her big mouth. We could tie her up," said Fetterman. "I tie very tight knots."

Jane squirmed. "You'd enjoy that, wouldn't you?"

Fetterman thought he detected a note of fear in her voice. "More likely you'd like it," he said. "I'd like to cut your throat, but I'll settle for tying you up."

Gerber grinned. "Serve her right if some of the NVA who ran off into the woods came back in and found her and had their way with her. But that still won't shut her up if relief troops get here before we're out of the country."

Fetterman brightened. "Say, uh, Jane dear. Tell us exactly what kind of medical supplies you've smuggled in for these needy human beings."

"Penicillin, bandages, adhesive tape, morphine—"

"Stop right there," said Fetterman, interrupting her. "So there you have it, Captain. We'll shoot her up with enough of her own morphine to knock her out for a few hours. Somehow it seems very appropriate."

IT WAS CLEARLY Russian radio gear. Bocker could tell from the Cyrillic characters stenciled in black above all of the knobs and the tuning dial. He jury-rigged a cable to connect the U.S.-made burst device to the transmitter that the North Vietnamese had been using to communicate with their troops in the South. When he had everything wired together he dialed up the correct frequency and began the procedure necessary to call up Nha Trang.

Bocker keyed the radio telegraph key. "Frosty Shadow, this is Frosty Ice, over."

He sighed with relief as Nha Trang came back almost at once. "Ice we read you five by five, over." Net control had picked up his Morse code signal loud and clear. They were halfway home.

Bocker whooped with unbridled joy. He had made contact at last. Perhaps their luck had changed for the better. "Get ready to copy our encrypted text, over." He had alerted them that he was about to transmit a message.

"Roger that. Go."

Bocker touched the button and the burst device's little tape whirled, sending out the details of what they had done so far and when and where behind the lines the helicopter could pick them up. He pushed back on the chair and waited for them to decipher his message. He found himself wondering how the brass would react when they found out he was sending classified messages from a captured radio station deep in the heart of North Vietnam.

After a few moments his reverie was broken by Nha Trang's terse reply. They had decrypted his message and encrypted their own response. Bocker hunched over the desk with the one-time pad in hand and penciled in the characters as they came across. "Short message," he said, with a trace of puzzlement in his voice. He had only copied four groups. In a matter of moments he had decrypted the communication. His jaw dropped in a mock expression when he read it. "Gee, why didn't we think of that?" he said dourly.

He handed the sheet of paper to Gerber, who read its contents aloud. "Steal the code books. Very creative. What do they think we are, mindless idiots?"

With their exfiltration place and time established, they had no further use for the enemy radio, so Gerber directed Bocker to set about sabotaging all of the electronic gear installed in the radio shack. Kai helped yank the access panel off the back of the transmitter and they shattered all of the vacuum tubes with the wooden butt of the dead radio operator's SKS carbine. That project completed, Bocker took the assault rifle and at point-blank range fired a single bullet through the power supply's bricklike transformer.

The Yard giggled at the destructive deed. "*Xin loi.* NVA be real pissed we wreck radio."

"*Xin loi,*" said Bocker.

They went outside to the generator and teamed up with Dirty Shirt, who offered to lend a hand. "You wanna torch the diesel fuel or just dump it out onto the ground?" he asked.

Bocker spoke with mock seriousness. "Shame on you, Staff Sergeant. Where is your concern for the environment? Maybe you should trot on inside and spend some quality time with Jane pinko and let her update you on all the right social concerns." Now he was smiling. "No, seriously, Shirt, I have a much better idea. We'll pour fifty pounds of sugar into the storage tank. They'll never know we dosed it with nasty stuff until they fuel up a few trucks and the pistons freeze in their bores. It will give 'em fits until they figure out what's gone wrong. Maybe a few of the trucks will give up the ghost out in the open and the Phantom jets will pick their bones clean."

"Uh-huh," said Shirt skeptically. "Good idea, oh esteemed sergeant, you with this splendiferous knowledge for wreaking havoc and destruction on enemy war supplies by expedient means. The wise men at the JFK center for unconventional warfare have taught you well. Only where you going to get the fucking sugar? You want I should make a run to the grocery store? Anything else we need, a loaf of bread, a six-pack, some toilet paper and napkins?''

Bocker enjoyed the good-natured kidding. ''Kindly go fuck yourself, Shirt. You ever look closely at a zip's gray, rotting teeth? Rest assured we'll find a basic load of sugar in their mess hall. They drink their coffee so sweet it melts the enamel clean off the molars. Only better take Kai with you on this quest, you wouldn't recognize the sweet stuff if you saw it, they eat it unrefined. Looks like a cross between brown sugar and salt.''

Bocker walked up to the diesel generator, ignoring the fact that it was running at full bore. As coolly as if he were tuning up the family station wagon in the driveway, he twirled off a wing nut, lifted up the air filter cover and pulled out the paper element. Then he opened a jerrican and, grunting with the strain, hoisted it shoulder high and began pouring a steady stream of diesel fuel down the generator set's air intake. Almost immediately the engine started a loud clanking and banging. Suddenly it screeched as if its metal parts had been clawed apart inside. It stopped all at once and a cloud of black smoke billowed ominously out of the exhaust pipe. The generator was enveloped in a cloud of smoke.

Gerber and Fetterman came running over. ''Jesus, what did you do to that thing?'' asked Fetterman, wide-eyed.

Bocker's grin stretched a mile wide. ''Simple law of physics. Fluid doesn't compress. Pouring diesel fuel down the air intake fills the cylinder with incompressible fluid. When the pistons came up, it bent the connecting rods. Boneyard for this baby. No more amps, watts or volts for the war effort.''

Gerber gave him a look of admiration. "How did you know how to do that? Street smarts or what?"

Bocker shook his head. "Little black book the CIA gave us. Ours is back in the team room. Remind me when we get back to camp. I'll show you. Lots of boffo stuff in there. You should be nicer to Maxwell. He can be very helpful with this sneaky stuff. He's really into it."

"You enjoy this kind of thing, don't you?" said Gerber.

Bocker shrugged in reply. "Hell, who doesn't? And you know what, Captain, we could burn down the buildings. If you want to."

Gerber laughed. "Okay, go ahead. And does Sergeant Bocker have any ideas about how to accomplish that task in military manner?"

"How about Molotov cocktails?" suggested Bocker. "I'll only take a minute."

Gerber looked on as Bocker used his knife to stir a mixture of sugar, rice husks, potassium chlorate and gasoline in a metal pail. Bocker was squatted next to a circle of quart-size brown bottles and the starting battery from the diesel generator. He uncorked the bottles one at a time and poured the contents onto the ground. He wrinkled his nose. "Whew. Vintage last Thursday."

"Seems like a perfectly good waste of *nouc mam*," said Gerber.

When all of the bottles were emptied, Bocker busied himself refilling them with the doctored gasoline and recorking them.

"I understand the principle of the Molotov cocktail," said Gerber. "But why the sugar, and why did you need that potassium chlorate from the zip dispensary?"

Bocker capped the last bottle. "The sugar jells the gasoline a little bit, makes it sticky, if you catch my drift. You know, like napalm. Sticky as in clings to whatever it lands on." He reached for the truck battery. One by one he unscrewed the little red caps spread across its top and neatly lined them up on the ground. That done, he grabbed the battery with both hands and tipped it over onto its side, purposely spilling electrolyte onto a wad of rags. Once they were thoroughly saturated with battery acid, he tied a rag tightly around each one of the bottle necks. Bocker anticipated Gerber's next question. "All you have to do is throw the bottle, it breaks on impact and the gasoline spills out. The sulfuric acid makes contact with the potassium chlorate, reacts and ignites the gasoline."

Gerber nodded. "And that way you don't have to fuck with lighting the wick and singeing off your own eyebrows."

Bocker grinned evilly. "Or worse." He got to his feet and wiped his hands down the front of his trousers. "There now. We can torch the buildings and they'll stay burning."

Suddenly Gerber cranked his head toward the barracks. "What's that sound?" he asked, crouching low.

Bocker gulped as he recognized the muffled sound of a tank engine. He looked to Gerber. "Don't say it. I know, I should have wired the tanks so they would blow up. Looks like I outsmarted myself."

"That doesn't matter now," said the captain, grabbing one of the freshly made Molotovs in each hand. "Come on, Galvin. We've got to knock the tank out."

The tank came at them with a roar. Following it were a squad of bedraggled NVA intent on wiping out the Americans and avenging the deaths of their comrades. Gerber figured they must have been survivors who had slipped off into the trees and regrouped.

The PT-76 came at them straight down the road that led from the barracks to the headquarters building. There was no cover and no way to get at the tank. Gerber and Bocker did the only prudent thing, retreated indoors.

Fetterman and the others met them just inside the door. Gerber immediately took charge of the situation. "Dirty Shirt and Kai, open fire on them through the windows. Keep moving so they can't zero in on you. Master Sergeant, you and Krung head out the back door, try to keep the ground troops busy. Come on, Galvin, we're going upstairs."

By now the tank had rolled directly in front of the building and started raking the ground floor with its machine gun. It fired its main battery once, splintering a hole through the wall between two windows. It almost looked comical as the commander hit the controls to rotate the turret, grinding the gears that wouldn't mesh. It took him only a moment to figure what was wrong. The driver wheeled the vehicle to one side, positioning it to fire another round from its main gun.

Hidden around the corner, Krung stripped a hand grenade from his webgear, pulled the pin and threw it as hard and as far as he could. Then he curled up into a tight ball and waited for it to go off. It detonated in the middle of a group of NVA, rolling clouds of white and orange smoking dust across the ground. The exploding shrapnel dropped one of the NVA soldiers. One of his legs became detached from his body and flew through the air to plop into the dirt. Krung fed a fresh magazine into his weapon and screamed at the top of his voice, "Die Commie motherfucker. Die."

Fetterman emptied his M-3 into three men who were running for cover behind a burning jeep. The slugs knocked them off their feet, nearly cutting the lead man in two.

The remaining NVA fanned out, trying to flank Fetterman. Waves of automatic fire from Soviet-built AK-47 rifles cracked overhead. An unseen enemy in the underbrush had pinned down Fetterman, Krung and Kai. Fetterman fired back instinctively in the direction of the reports with short bursts from his own M-3. He couldn't see the target, but he knew it was best to respond with as much firepower as possible. Another hidden NVA trooper fired an RPG. It exploded barely twenty meters away. Right range, wrong windage, mused Fetterman. Next one would likely be right on target.

The PT-76 charged forward, ramming its nose into the front door and then screeching to a halt. A swarm of NVA scrambled to their feet and started firing into the building. A brown bottle dropped out of a second-story window and shattered, splashing liquid over the turret. A split second later an audible whump signaled that the flames had ignited, and three more bottles came crashing down from Gerber and Bocker's hands. The flames spread down the back of the tank and ignited the fuel cells.

"Now!" yelled Bocker.

Suddenly Fetterman was on his feet, sprinting forward with his submachine gun chattering. Bulldozing his way through the brush along the edge of the tree line, he was trying to gain the enemy's flank.

Krung jumped to his feet to follow Fetterman. The two of them fired into the brush and ground cover that concealed the enemy. A flurry of hand grenades detonated where the men had been lying just moments before, severing some of the antenna guy wires. Krung pulled the trigger, his gun bucked twice in his hands and then jammed. Krung swore as he fell to the ground and worked to clear the jammed shell casing.

Fetterman spotted the brilliant orange muzzle-flash of an AK-47. He fell to the ground, rolled onto his back, yanked the pin from a grenade and hurled it, ending the NVA attempt to flank their position.

From the second story, Gerber fired twice more, picking off another pair of slow-moving soldiers. The NVA small-arms fire crackled and then fell silent as Fetterman wiped out the last defenders for the second time in six hours.

12

RADIO RESEARCH FACILITY, PHU BAI SOUTH VIETNAM

Even though working the midnight shift screwed up his sleep patterns so much that he always felt tired and irritable, Specialist Davis liked mids. Around 1800 hours the lifers made a mass exodus from the field station. By the time Davis came on duty all the field-grade brass and the E-8s were sound asleep in their quarters. Nothing ever happened on mids.

Usually between midnight and seven in the morning the traffic they copied was as predictable as the sunrise. And if the lifers left word that the operators were supposed to increase production by intercepting additional encrypted transmissions to compete with other units in Vietnam, they'd comply by padding their copy, by typing in random letters and special characters and then chuckle at the thought of the cryptographers trying to break the bogus cipher.

But this morning it was different. Unbelievably Spec Four Davis had lost his NVA man at Phu Tho. One minute he had been in the middle of a code group, intercepting what looked like a routine message and all of a sudden the transmission stopped cold. He shifted uncomfortably in his chair. It had never happened before. Fearing a frequency change, a stunned Davis waited only a few minutes before beginning to sweep the dial across the most likely frequencies, but to no avail.

Six hours later he breathed a premature sigh of relief when the oscilloscope fingerprinted the NVA transmitter, but something was different. The code groups he copied were coming across faster, at about eighteen groups per minute, nearly twice as fast as his man had ever sent.

Even more peculiar was that each character was keyed crisply and clean. Without a doubt they had changed operators. Davis wondered why. And then even more mysteriously the code speed spurted from eighteen groups per minute to about four hundred. Trained intercept operator that he was, Davis recognized it as a burst transmission. This was significant stuff. "Oh, shit," he yelled with excitement. And then he called for the trick chief.

The NCO stood behind Davis's position, "Whatcha got for me here, Specialist?"

"This is weird, I think we should call a CRITIC." Then the bewildered intercept operator explained what had happened.

The NCO took the earphones, but by now the station was off the air again. He handed the headset back to Davis. "You're sure it was a burst device?"

The two men looked at each other for a moment. Davis came out with it first. "You don't suppose that was an American transmission out of North Vietnam, do you?"

The NCO didn't answer for a moment, as he considered how to handle the situation. Finally he said,

"Davis, you remember when you joined the agency and they did the background investigation on you? How the guys in the suits talked to your mom and dad, the neighbors, your teachers at school and the minister?"

Davis nodded. "Yeah, everybody thought it was the cops checking up on me because I had murdered somebody or stolen something."

The NCO went on. "And you remember that little piece of paper you signed when they gave you the top secret crypto clearance and the piece of paper said you agreed to keep your mouth shut about classified information?"

"Yeah, yeah, right. Come on, Sergeant. Get on with it already."

The NCO laid a hand on the specialist's shoulder. "What you heard tonight is classified and you don't talk to anybody about it. In fact, grab your stuff and let's go talk to the major."

A MOIST BREEZE BLEW in off the South China Sea as Marine Corps Major Oliver Brooks made his way to the briefing room at the U.S. air base at Da Nang. The wind tugging at his back carried the familiar smell of jet engine exhaust to his nostrils; the odor quickened his pulse as he heard the jet engine start cart whining away.

Once inside Brooks, his RIO and the other flight crew gathered in operations for the briefing on the rules of engagement, which were in constant flux. After takeoff, the two aircraft were to proceed up the coast to rendezvous with a KC130F tanker to take on fuel. After the air refueling was complete, he and his wingman were to cross the coastline slightly north of the DMZ. Brooks would try to draw some MiGs out of Phuc Yen airfield east of Hanoi and try to shoot them down. Simple enough in theory, thought Brooks. He had done it dozens of times before during this tour and the one previous. But in this war he had quickly learned that all constants were variable.

His wingman on the seek-and-destroy mission was Captain Bob Barnett who was one up on Brooks with three tours of duty in Vietnam. But Captain Barnett never brought up the topic unless asked; he was very modest about it all. Brooks chuckled when he thought about it, and could see Barnett back in the States acting so humble that it would be easy to entertain the notion that he had never even been in the military.

Brooks suited up. First was the flight suit, followed by the G-suit. It was essentially an inflatable girdle that covered abdomen, thighs and calves. Laced tight and inflated, it prevented blood flowing from the torso into the abdomen and legs. Anytime the pilot pulled more than 2.5 Gs, the suit automatically inflated to keep blood from pooling below the waist. That was important because without enough blood to supply oxygen to the gray matter, the brain blacked out and the plane crashed.

Brooks walked into the line shack and picked up his yellow sheet. He wondered why they called them yellow sheets when they were never yellow.

The pilot and the RIO walked to the flight line. Their aircraft was Alpha Bravo Eight, a beat-up F-4D Phantom with patches of zinc chromate primer blotching the skin where holes in the fuselage and wings had been patched. Alpha Bravo Eight was configured with a six-hundred-gallon centerline fuel tank, four Sparrow and four Sidewinder missiles. With the Sparrow, the Phantom's radar would paint the target and tell the missile where to find it. The Sidewinder was a heat-seeking missile that would home in on the infrared heat of a jet engine. It was the job of his RIO, also affectionately known as the guy in back, to operate the air-to-air weapons system.

Brooks climbed into the cockpit, which reeked of sweat, mildew, hydraulic fluid and fried wiring. With the help of the start cart, the pilot fired up the Phantom. After he was satisfied that the right engine was spooled up to idle, he repeated the start procedure for the left engine.

Brooks keyed the mike. "Da Nang Ground, Hurricane One taxi for two. Request blocktimes zero-zero, four-zero and four-four." Hurricane was the flight's tactical call signs. The blocktimes were prearranged so planes could make an approach to Da Nang if their radios went out. If Brooks's radio went dead he was automatically cleared to land at 7:40 and 7:44 local time. All other flights would be routed out of the way.

The tower came back. "Hurricane one, cleared runway three-five, winds zero-four-five at one-one, gusting one-five. Altimeter two-niner point eight-nine. Blocktimes zero-zero, four-zero and four-four confirmed."

Just before the head of the runway they came to the arming area where the missiles were plugged into their firing circuits. Red strips of canvas fluttered from the armament of the F-4D Phantom jet as he taxied to the end of the runway for a takeoff from Da Nang.

At the end of each strip was the safety pin that armed the missiles. An ordnance man ducked beneath the wings and plucked off the brightly colored strips and made the necessary connections to the firing circuits. Finished, and with an exaggerated motion he held out the ribbons to show to the pilot. Each of the four radar-guided Sparrow and heat-seeking Sidewinder missiles were now armed and dangerous.

"Skidrow One, ready for takeoff."

"Skidrow One, flight cleared for takeoff. Maintain runway heading. Contact departure control on button four when safely airborne."

Brooks and his wingman wheeled onto the runway. They ran up the engines, accelerating from idle to 100 percent. The wingman signaled thumbs-up.

Brooks threw the throttles forward, accelerating through 80 percent RPM. He released the wheel brakes. The plane gained momentum. He selected afterburners and engine thrust jumped. The runway markers began to gallop past as the airspeed needle wound up. The wheels thumped and thudded, rocking the plane from side to side and then the ride smoothed.

Flaps up, gear up, they climbed. At 300 knots Brooks backed off on the afterburners in an effort to save fuel and wear on the engine. The Phantom climbed at 2,000 feet per minute. After ten minutes and seventy miles they leveled off at 21,500 feet and headed for North Vietnam.

See the enemy before he sees you. The dogfighter's credo was running through Brooks's mind the very moment two blips appeared on the edge of the radarscope. On the ground, Brooks could see a ring of 57 mm anti-aircraft cannon guarding a bridge. As he flew over, the North Vietnamese gunners with the Russian advisers lofted shells at him. Cotton ball puffs of smoke from the flak battery dotted the sky but did no damage to his airplane.

A little farther into the flight Brooks noticed an unfinished SAM site on the ground, its distinctive layout easily recognizable after his studies of aerial photographs of the rockets on their launchers with the paved roads that led up to their firing pads. He made a note to report the partially completed site during debriefing.

A warning light flashed in the cockpit and the sensor emitted a loud burst of static like a diamondback rattling its tail as enemy radar locked onto his Phantom. Operational SAM site, he corrected himself. He waited for the turkeys on the ground to launch the SAM, betting that he could outmaneuver the thirty-five-foot long, two-stage rocket as it streaked toward him.

He saw the launch, and the steam. The Russian-built SA-2 went straight up for a while and then the booster dropped off. Brooks knew the split-second timing of the maneuver he was about to make was crucial. If he dodged the missile prematurely, it would turn and catch up. On the other hand, if he waited too long before beginning the maneuver, the 340-pound warhead would explode near enough to his aircraft to knock him out of the sky. He considered it to be roughly akin to an airborne game of chicken.

His reflexes were keenly honed. At just the right moment he poked the nose down. The SAM followed. Then he pulled up as hard as he could and took off, the missile streaking below. He breathed a sigh of relief.

Moments later a MiG popped out of the clouds. Brooks turned the F-4 to engage it, noting the skies were now swarming with fighters launched from Phuc Yen airfield. Brooks pulled sharp right and barrel-rolled to the left, holding his position above and behind the first MiG. Now in range, he completed the rolling maneuver and fell in behind and below the MiG. He squeezed the trigger. The first Sparrow passed wide, the second hit just behind the canopy, cutting the plane in two and turning the MiG into a gout of orange flame.

Brooks's wingman, Barnett, spotted a second MiG and told his back seat first lieutenant to lock the Phantom's radar onto it. Seconds later the guy in back launched two Sparrow missiles in close succession. Uncharacteristically, Barnett had eased too close to the target and both missiles missed. In frustration, he pulled his Phantom into a climbing left turn that put him directly behind the MiG.

Without warning, Barnett's F-4 heaved and crumpled; an Atoll missile had sneaked up on them. Somehow Barnett managed to pop the canopy and ejected safely. After he cleared the seat he looked up to see his multicolored parachute canopy mushroomed against the sky. He watched as his falling plane exploded into an orange fireball.

Barnett came down in a clearing, landing hard enough to knock the wind out of him. After he caught his breath, he gathered up the canopy so the white and orange panels weren't showing, and ditched it behind a bush. He was pleased to see the OD nylon panels would blend in nicely with the foliage and would be nearly impossible to see unless an NVA trooper stepped on it.

Barnett heard voices and took off down a trail, sprinting as fast as he could. He walked for a while, catching his breath, until he came to an intersecting trail. Then he took off again at a lope, running for what seemed to be a lifetime. He tripped and plunged through a tangle of undergrowth, picked himself up and plodded on. Finally, unable to go any farther, he threw himself into a clump of bushes.

13

AIR COMBAT
SOMEWHERE IN NORTH
VIETNAM

All they had to do was last out the day. They had made it to the LZ where the helicopter would come at dusk when the light would be poor. Gerber wanted it that way because then the helicopter could swoop in to exfiltrate them as they made their escape into the shadows of the night. So Gerber's recon team waited.

The flat ricelands stretched for miles. In the middle of the paddy directly in front of Gerber, a domesticated water buffalo used his crescent-shaped horns as a shovel. The huge, bulky animal dipped his horns into the mud, bent backward and with a sideways flick of his massive head threw dollops of watery mud onto his back. Then he lay on his belly, and beating his front legs, splashed fresh mud on his body.

When the early-morning stillness was broken by the far-off roar of jet planes, Gerber unlimbered his binoculars and began to search the blue sky for the source of the feeble noise.

After a few moments he found two tiny black dots on the horizon looming larger by the moment. In fascination he watched as two fighter planes, one an enemy MiG and one a friendly Phantom, twisted and turned, chasing each other through the puffy white clouds. He recognized the Phantom jet by its upturned wings and downturned nose. The MiG, with its bright red star and swept-back wings was of Korean War vintage, so it, too, was no stranger to his recollection.

Each one of the fighter planes tried to get an angle on the other. Both jets' afterburners trailed black smoke as they climbed to higher altitudes where they sorted out textbook tactics. Fetterman and Bocker shamelessly oohed and aahed as if they were watching a Fourth of July fireworks show back at the country fair instead of a life-and-death battle three miles high. To Gerber it seemed that the Phantom was losing, but it ended badly for the MiG-17.

Without warning, the Phantom barrel-rolled and fell in behind the MiG. The Russian fighter clawed at the sky, trying to gain altitude and correct his horrible mistake. Gerber watched in fascination as the American jet jock launched a missile that flew right up the tail section of the MiG and melted the wax from its wings. There was a bright yellow flash as it detonated, knocking the tail section off the fuselage. A moment later the muffled bang reached Gerber. "Where is he? Did he eject?"

A minute passed and then Dirty Shirt pointed excitedly toward the sky. "There. There he is." They all watched as a white canopy spilled out of its pack tray and then inflated as the MiG pilot parachuted to earth.

The empty MiG fell, twisting, corkscrewing and tumbling lazily toward the ground. Finally it erupted in a brilliant flash of orange flame. Broken bits and pieces tumbled lazily from the clouds.

Fetterman watched the white parachute float ever so slowly to earth. One hundred feet off the ground, they could see the pilot as he visibly braced for a landing. It was a textbook parachute landing fall: feet and knees together, the pilot landed on the balls of his feet and rolled off to one side, breaking the fall. He got up, dusted himself off and a moment later the downed enemy pilot was daisy-chaining the billowing chute in his arms. They could hear him whistling. And that wasn't so incredible. After all, he wasn't behind enemy lines and he probably had it figured that he wouldn't even miss a meal. At least he was alive.

But the American pilot wasn't through with him yet. Like a vulture circling for a kill, he bled off altitude and swooped his F-4 Phantom right down to the deck and so close to the dirt that Gerber was able to differentiate between the three shades of green in the Vietnam theater camouflage. He could read the USMC tail code that identified it as a plane out of Da Nang. In awe, Gerber looked inside the Plexiglas canopy as the pilot turned his head and waved his black-gloved hand at his downed foe.

"That a boy. Rub his nose in it," said Bocker. "Rub his nose in it real good."

"OK, jarhead," said Gerber with a chuckle. "I'm suitably impressed. Now what?" Gerber could sense the Marine Corps pilot's unbridled youth. He was a young man, probably twenty-seven or twenty-eight years old, an Annapolis graduate who had burned up long nights studying swept wing geometry, and supersonic air vortices before the brass in the gold braid and white uniforms allowed him to fly millions of dollars' worth of aluminum and electronic gear at twice the speed of sound.

But the zoomie still wasn't finished. Low as before, he climbed and circled the rice paddy in a long, slow turn. Coming down his plane streamed vapor trails; he swooped in close and unleashed another missile.

Thinking it was aimed at him, the downed pilot leaped into the air, whirled and started tromping through the mud, making a mad dash for the tree line.

The first time around the sound of the plane had startled the water buffalo. Now with the plane on the second run, the beast ran clumsily in the mud and seemingly without direction.

Gerber's and Bocker's jaws dropped when they realized what the pilot's target was.

The world downshifted into slow motion. Gerber and Bocker watched in absolute horror as the missile homed in on its flesh-and-blood target. The warhead buried itself dead center between the water buffalo's buttocks. There was a flash of very bright light followed by a bloody mist. Bang. No more water buffalo.

Bocker rolled on the ground, laughing. "Teach the goddamn water buffalo to fart with a heat-seeking missile in the area."

The Phantom jet climbed, circled to the east and disappeared over the horizon, leaving a wisp of smoke as the only clue that he had been there. That, the downed pilot and a bloody pile of gore in the middle of the paddy.

Coated with mud from head to toe, the downed pilot had stopped running. Facing the east, he looked at the departed Phantom and shook his fist at it.

Gerber turned to Fetterman. "What do you think?"

Fetterman shrugged. "If we capture him we could take him back with us for debriefing. If we kill him and they find the body, they'll know we're here and come looking for us." He paused for a moment. "But we could always hide the body. Stuff him in the mud or something."

Bocker said, "Or we could always close our eyes and let him walk away."

The four Americans looked at one another. "Nah," they said in unison.

Gerber used hand signals to deploy Krung and Kai.

The two men walked nonchalantly toward the downed pilot, talking in subdued tones. "He not Vietnamese," whispered Krung. "I think he Russian."

"How can you tell?" asked Kai.

"His smell. He smell different. Like the Americans."

Kai giggled. "Maybe that's the water buffalo you smell, not the pilot."

The downed pilot noticed the AK-47s, Kai and Krung's Oriental build, and naturally assumed them to be North Vietnamese rescuers whose job it was to escort him back to Phuc Yen air base. He smiled and said something condescending in Vietnamese.

Neither Krung nor Kai smiled back. They were close enough to tell that Krung had been right, he was a lend-lease Russian pilot. Now face-to-face with him, Krung jabbed a gun barrel in his stomach. The smile faded as the pilot jabbered away. Neither Krung nor Kai answered his protestations. He lost his command of Vietnamese and broke into Russian.

Finally, he pressed both hands together and kowtowed to the two of them. They escorted him to the tree line. When the downed pilot saw Gerber and Fetterman, a quizzical expression swept over his face followed by one of sheer panic.

"I don't know what he's worried about," said Fetterman. "We're not going to hurt him. We're just going to kill him a little bit."

Without warning, Krung swung the wooden butt of his AK across the pilot's skull, knocking him cold. The pilot crumpled. After a minute or so, he came to and sat up, shaking his head. He blinked, saw the look of hate etched onto Krung's face, gulped hard, then shut his eyes again. Kai reached down, grabbed him by the arm and roughly pulled him to his feet.

The pilot opened his eyes and reached into a vest pocket of his flight suit. In one sweeping motion he pulled out an automatic pistol and shot Kai.

The edge of a rice paddy is a horrible place to die. The Russian's bullet had caught Kai in the throat and came out the back of his head. "I'm hit," screamed Kai, as he crumpled in pain. "I'm hit, I'm going to die."

In reflex action Krung fired off three quick shots, spinning the pilot around. The Russian looked stunned as he fell to the ground and began to cough up blood. The red liquid oozed from the three black-ringed holes evenly spaced across his chest. The blood quickly drained from his arteries, coagulating in the mud. Teeth gritted, he covered the gushing chest wound as pink froth bubbled in his fingers. The dead Russian's heart continued to pump for a while after his passing, spraying even more blood at his feet.

The wounded Montagnard was a bloody sight. He lay flat on his back, supported by Bocker. The sergeant felt his weight on top of him and heard his labored breathing. The American held Kai's head sideways so that if he threw up he wouldn't choke to death on his own vomit. He knew wounded men vomit a lot when headshot. Miraculously Kai was still alive. Obviously in great pain he had chewed his fingers until they bled to keep from screaming. Fading fast, he groaned and fought, thrashing from side to side. He tried to sit upright but the struggling made him bleed all the more.

With furrowed brow, Krung stood over Kai and asked, "Do you think he die before helicopter come?"

Bocker gazed at Kai's waxen face for a moment before answering. "It's hard to say. A man can live a long time with a wound like that." Bocker's mouth felt as dry as sand.

Krung sank to his knees beside the wounded man. "You be all right," he told him in a hushed voice. "Not time to die. Not kill enough VC."

A that moment Kai sat up with a great trembling motion, then slumped over and was dead. Taut with frustration, Bocker drew his fingers into a tight fist, then released them. He rolled Kai over onto his back and opened the top button of the Montagnard's shirt. He pulled out the gold Buddha and tenderly placed it inside the wiry man's mouth. "This is a lousy mission," grunted Bocker. "Lousy."

They divided up Kai's ammunition and smashed his AK against a tree, rendering it useless. Gerber, Bocker, Fetterman and Krung stood over Kai. His body was still limp and warm. They stood quietly for a few moments.

"Go on. Say it," Gerber heard someone whisper.

He felt his scalp tingle. He drew a breath to speak. "Life is a great circular movement." He paused for a moment. "The circle is the most perfect geometric pattern. It lacks nothing. Inside the circle complete balance reigns."

Then it was Fetterman's turn. "*Memento mori.* Remember, you must die."

ALMOST AS SOON AS Barnett was on the ground, the NVA were upon him. At first the downed American pilot had run like a frightened deer, smashing and crashing through the brush. But in the end, his legs cramped and unable to catch his wind, he gave up. Two NVA soldiers laughed as they grabbed him by the wrists, dragging him out into the clearing and dumping him in front of a waiting Bao.

Arms folded across his chest, Bao directed the men to hold him on the ground by his arms and legs. Bao laid the toe of his boot on the pilot's chest and slowly drew his knife from its sheath. With a grin devoid of mirth he waved the knife blade back and forth in front of the pilot's face, the razor-sharp blade glinting in the rays of sunlight. He wanted the pilot to know what fate had befallen him. When he tired of waving the knife, Bao sat down on the American's legs, reached for his chest and grabbed a handful of the flight coverall.

The American's eyes grew wide in terror. He gulped, closed his eyes and said nothing.

Bao grinned evilly and lowered the knife. Again and again he slashed away, holding the knife in one hand, and pulled away hunks of flight suit and brass zipper with the other. Soon the American lay there, naked in the sun, blood trickling from a dozen slashes where the carelessly wielded blade had cut flesh as well as flight suit fabric.

Now Bao stood over the American pilot and pointed an accusing finger. "War criminal. You drop bombs and kill innocent women and children," said Bao in his singsong voice. "Now you will pay."

Like a surgeon cutting for the very first time, Bao jabbed the tip of his knife just below the man's sternum and slowly drew the edge of the blade down the belly. He cut from sternum to groin, the tip of the blade barely penetrating the skin, muscle and viscera, laying Barnett wide open, exposing the internal organs.

"Flip him over onto side," shrieked Bao in an excited voice. His nostrils were flared, his pulse beat fast as he laid down the knife.

Up to that point, the American hadn't cried out. Now he howled in unashamed pain. The howling sounded strange because it was uttered from a blood-filled mouth clogged with a mangled tongue that he had nearly bitten clean through to keep from screaming. He hadn't wanted to give the enemy the satisfaction of breaking him.

Bao squatted beside the man, reached into the mass of guts, grabbed a length of bowel and started squeezing. Methodically he worked his way down the large intestine, milking the length of it.

Some of the North Vietnamese who were holding down the pilot paled and turned away. One man stumbled off into the bushes and vomited. The others laughed and joked as Bao literally squeezed the shit out of the American.

When Bao was finished, he wiped his bloodied hands on the pilot's buttocks. With a look of disgust on his face, the American gathered his insides up in his arms and lay there panting.

Bao pulled the UHC-10 hand-held radio out of his back pocket and hurled it to the ground, shattering its case and scattering transistorized components and broken bits of circuit board in the dirt.

Bao and the others turned their backs on him and slowly walked away. Bao paused for a moment, looked over his shoulder and called back to the man who writhed on the ground. "Hey, American war criminal. If you can crawl eighty miles to the coast, a helicopter will rescue you." Bao came to rigid attention, saluted and walked away.

14

RADIO RESEARCH
FACILITY, PHU BAI

Working the midnight shift at the ASA Field Station near Phu Bai, Spec Four Davis sat in front of his Collins R-390 shortwave receiver, patiently listening for the distinctive di-dah-dits of a particular North Vietnamese radio operator. Davis adjusted the headset so it felt more comfortable on his ears and then began to whirl the big black frequency knob back and forth to hear better over the crackling static.

The trick chief walked along the row of intercept operators seated in front of R-390 radios. He stopped behind Davis and yawned. ''Ever find your phantom operator again?''

Davis didn't even bother to turn around, he just shook his head and kept searching. Davis was beginning to miss the nightly challenge of copying the garbled code. It was as if the faceless, nameless enemy radio operator had been a known commodity. In fact he felt a strange kinship with him. Often he found himself wondering what the guy looked like and whether he liked the North Vietnamese Army any better than he liked the U.S.

Army. And what was the meaning of that last strange transmission? He turned to the NCO. "Whatever happened to him? Did anybody at DIRNSA ever figure it out?"

The trick chief said, "We replayed that reel of tape, ran it through the oscilloscope once or twice. Checks out as the same transmitter, but definitely a different operator on the key." After a pause the trick chief tried to cheer him up. "The Russian and East German Army radio operators are well trained. When you intercept their code groups at least you can tell a dot from a dash."

Davis was on levy to go to Germany. He had enlisted for four years and had more than two left. And even though he had originally enlisted to go to Europe, the prospect of seeing the Black Forest while still in the Army left a sour taste in his mouth. "FTA," muttered Davis under his breath. Fuck the army.

"Say what? What did you say," the trick chief asked, not believing what he thought he had heard him say.

"Seventeen days and a wake-up," he said.

"You'll like Germany," the trick chief said. "Ever think of making a career of the Army?"

Davis whirled in his chair and glared at his NCO.

"Naw. I guess not." The trick chief moved down the line.

HALF AN HOUR before their station time with the helicopter, Gerber and his team walked out of the jungle and onto the dirt road that paralleled the rice paddy. Bocker took point and they trudged on for about ten minutes until they came to a clearing. A hundred meters into it they noticed the grass had been knocked down as if a number of men had been through before them. There were also several piles of steaming spoor that could only have been left by a very large animal.

Bocker and Gerber squatted next to each other and studied the evidence. Bocker was good at tracking. "From the grass that's knocked down flat, and the elephant tracks, and the amount of dung, I'd estimate about a battalion passed this way. Not long ago."

Krung shared his knowledge of wildlife. "NVA like elephants. They walk quiet. Ears more good than man."

"I've heard that before," said Dirty Shirt.

By then Bocker had found human footprints in the mud, the impressions evenly spaced with deep toe marks. "Whoever they are, they're carrying heavy loads and heading south."

"They probably picked up supplies here on their way to the Ho Chi Minh Trail," said Fetterman.

"How far behind them are we?" asked Gerber.

Bocker squinted at the sun, low on the horizon. "Oh, I don't know. Sometime early this morning, late yesterday. Somewhere in there. Near as I can tell."

"Let's figure the grid coordinates of this place and plot their route. During briefback we can turn it over to the Air Force and maybe they can call in an air strike on them. Too bad we don't have any claymores left or we could leave some booby traps. Doesn't really matter, since we've spotted the trail the intel guys can keep an eye on it." Out of the corner of his eye Gerber saw something metallic glinting in the sun. He squatted, careful not to disturb the foliage. He counted four 7.62 mm rounds, ammo that would chamber in both the AK-47 and the SKS carbine. Gerber snorted. "Ah, so the much vaunted NVA are fallible after all. In fact it would seem they're getting to be as careless as American troops."

The men spread out in a semblance of a skirmish line and searched the area. In the meantime Bocker had continued to poke around in the knocked-down grass and found three abandoned gourds and some grains of rice scattered on the ground, more evidence that enemy soldiers had passed that way.

On the other side of the clearing, Fetterman peered beneath a fallen tree and found what looked like a huge nest covered with dry grass and weeds. The scent of urine was strong in the air. And the tree bark had been scratched by what had to be a big set of sharp claws.

"Captain," called Fetterman, pointing to the nest.

"Tiger?" said Gerber, standing next to him now.

Out of curiosity more than anything else they walked on the trail. Nobody said anything. Fetterman spotted the tiger tracks first. He gave a low whistle. "Look at the size of these." Fingers splayed wide, he laid his hand down over the indent in the dirt. "His paws must be enormous."

"How big does that make him?" interrupted Gerber.

Bocker shrugged. "The cats get real big. Does it really matter how big this one is? Five hundred pounds, or a thousand, it just doesn't matter. If he clamps his teeth down on you, you're dead meat, plain and simple."

"He's obviously following the NVA. Is he stalking them?"

Bocker shrugged. "Tigers are real curious animals. Maybe he's pissed because they're stomping all over his territory. They're like that. Very territorial."

"So what's he doing, following them till they leave his area of operations?"

Bocker shook his head. "No. You're right, he's definitely stalking them."

"What I wouldn't give to see the look on their faces when he picks out his prey and grabs him by the nape of the neck and drags him off into the boonies."

Silently, Dirty Shirt stood over one of the piles of elephant droppings, staring down at it as if it held some fascination for him. "Hey, Bocker," he called in a monotone.

Bocker padded over. "Yeah, what's up?" His voice betrayed his puzzlement with Dirty Shirt's preoccupation with the excrement.

"You remember that MACV blowgut named Cassidy? The one that was threatening to kill that puppy?"

"Yeah."

"And how we agreed something ought to happen to that sumbitch?"

"Yeah, yeah. So what."

"So once we're exfiltrated we'll be passing through that limp dick's air base on our way back to Nha Trang." Dirty Shirt's eyes were twinkling as he looked from Bocker to the dung and back again.

Bocker's quizzical expression changed into a grin. Without a word the two men lowered their empty rucksacks to the ground, opened them wide and started kicking great wads of elephant dung into the compartment.

Gerber saw what they were doing and walked over, followed by Fetterman and Krung. Gerber didn't say a word, he just looked on as they gathered up clods of sweet-smelling dung.

"No doubt you're wondering what we're doing," said Shirt, never missing a beat.

Bocker breathlessly told him the story about Cassidy, the dog and the elephant.

Gerber glowered in remembrance, as he lowered his own rucksack to the ground and began to fill it with elephant dirt. "What the hell," he said. "We already smell ripe enough to be picked."

THE TIGER PADDED SILENTLY along the streambed, his tawny black-striped coat blending into the foliage. He stopped at a widening of the stream where myriad tiny animal tracks converged on the water's edge. Now lying motionless, his natural camouflage rendered him invisible to the human eye.

The tiger watched Bao's soldiers walking leisurely, with their rifles slung carelessly over their shoulders. He heard someone call them to a halt and then watched as the man who had called out left them to walk down the streambed and out of their sight.

The animal watched as the lone soldier poked his head out of the undergrowth and peered at the water hole. Satisfied that there was no imminent danger, the human scurried down to drink. Squatting in the mud at the water's edge, he cupped his hand in the water, then raised his head up and looked around before bringing his hand to his mouth. Thirst satisfied, he whirled and trotted over to a clump of bushes, unbuttoned his trousers and began to urinate.

The cat stalked closer and closer until he was within a few yards of his prey. Sensing something amiss, the man pricked up his ears and raised his head once. He jerked his head around to look to either side. Reassured that all was well, he returned his attention to what he was doing.

The tiger made his move. In a few steps he was on the man's back, using his weight and the strength of his massive forelegs to force him down onto the ground. The powerful cat reached one of his forearms around Bao and raked his sharp claws against the man's soft belly. The man screamed at the top of his lungs as he watched his internal organs spill to the ground. Tired of playing the game, the tiger bit the back of the man's neck, severing Bao's spine.

15

MAC SOG
HEADQUARTERS NEAR
TAN SON NHUT, SOUTH
VIETNAM

Gerber and recon team Frosty Shadow walked down a long hall somewhere in the middle of the headquarters building where they were due for the briefback. Keeping pace with Fetterman, Gerber was preoccupied with all that had happened in the past forty-eight hours, trying to recall all of the pertinent details the intel types would want to know about the mission, but especially the information on the Chinese Army officer and the Russian pilot. They would absorb the information, collate and assess it, and in the end it would probably result in another recon team infiltrating the North to act on whatever it was that they had learned.

Gerber hoped that whichever team infiltrated would have better luck finding their IP. Gerber made a mental note to keep his cool when he talked to the Air Force liaison officer about the fine art of airplane navigation.

Rounding a corner, Gerber bumped into Major Blauveldt, who seemed to be in an especially jovial mood. "Glad to see you guys in one piece. I wasn't all that sure you'd make it back," he said. "You'll be glad to know those tulips you've planted are already plugged into the system. Funny thing, though, there doesn't seem to be the level of activity up there that we anticipated. And that's strange, given the SID row's proximity to the supply depot." He stuck out a finger and counted heads. "Wait a minute," he said with some concern. "You're one man short. Where's the sixth member of your team?"

"Dead," said Gerber. "Kai joined the ghost army."

"That's too bad," said Blauveldt. His voice had taken on a more somber tone and his smile had faded. "I'm sorry to hear we lost a good man."

Krung nodded. "Yes. Too bad. Him good shot. Kill many VC. I avenge his death. Kill fifty VC for Kai. Swear do this on his grave."

"I'm sure you will," Blauveldt said slowly. "I'm sure you will."

Bocker held out the aluminum briefcase and handed it to Blauveldt. "Here. Thought you might want this back."

Blauveldt took it and frowned as he noticed dozens of little dents in its metal skin that hadn't been there a week before. "So, how'd it work? That radio gear in there worth a flying fuck? Save your ass like I said it would?"

Bocker shrugged. "Nah. In fact, we never even had a chance to turn it on. But I sure felt important as hell walking around in the jungle with a briefcase."

GLOSSARY

AC—Aircraft Commander. The pilot in charge of the aircraft.

ADO—A-Detachment's area of operations.

AFVN—Armed Forces radio and television network in Vietnam. Army PFC Pat Sajak was probably the most memorable of AFVN's DJs with his loud and long, "GOOOOOOOOOOOOOD MORNing, Vietnam!" The spinning Wheel of Fortune gives no clues about his whereabouts today.

AK-47—Assault rifle normally used by the North Vietnamese and the Vietcong.

AO—Area of Operations.

AO DAI—Long dresslike garment, split up the sides and worn over pants.

AP ROUNDS—Armor-piercing ammunition.

APU—Auxiliary Power Unit. An outside source of power used to start aircraft engines.

ARC LIGHT—Term used for a B-52 bombing mission. It was also known as heavy arty.

ARVN—Army of the Republic of Vietnam. A South Vietnamese soldier. Also known as Marvin Arvin.

ASA—Army Security Agency. Electronic intelligence gatherers.

AST—Control officer between men in isolation and the outside world. He is responsible for taking care of all problems.

AUTOVON—Army phone system that allowed soldiers on one base to call another base, bypassing the civilian phone system.

BISCUIT—C-rations.

BODY COUNT—Number of enemy killed, wounded or captured during an operation. Used by Saigon and Washington as a means of measuring progress of the war.

BOOM-BOOM—Term used by Vietnamese prostitutes in selling their services.

BOONDOGGLE—Any military operation that hasn't been completely thought out. An operation that is ridiculous.

BOONIE HAT—Soft cap worn by a grunt in the field when he wasn't wearing his steel pot.

BREAK STARCH—Don fresh starched fatigues.

BUSHMASTER—Jungle warfare expert or soldier skilled in jungle navigation. Also a deadly snake not common to Vietnam but mighty tasty.

C AND C—Command and Control aircraft that circled overhead to direct combined air and ground operations.

CAO BOIS—(cowboys) Term that referred to the criminals of Saigon who rode motorcycles.

CARIBOU—Cargo transport plane.

CHINOOK—Army Aviation twin-engine helicopter. A CH-47. See also SHIT HOOK.

CHOCK—Term referring to the number of the aircraft in the flight. Chock Three was the third. Chock Six was the sixth.

CLAYMORE—Antipersonnel mine that fires seven hundred and fifty steel balls with a lethal range of fifty meters.

CLOSE AIR SUPPORT—Use of airplanes and helicopters to fire on enemy units near friendly troops.

CO CONG—Female Vietcong.

CONEX—Steel container about ten feet height, ten feet deep and ten feet long used to haul equipment and supplies.

CRITIC—

DAI UY—Vietnamese army rank, the equivalent of captain.

DEROS—Date of estimated return from overseas.

DF—Direction Finder.

DIRNSA—Director, National Security Agency.

E-6—Staff Sergeant.

E AND E—Escape and evasion.

FAC—Forward air controller.

FEET WET—Term used by pilots to describe flight over water.

FIVE—Radio call sign for the executive officer of a unit.

FNG—Fucking new guy.

FOB—Forward operating base.

FOX MIKE—FM radio.

FREEDOM BIRD—Name given to any aircraft that took troops out of Vietnam. Usually referred to the commercial jet flights that took men back to the World.

GARAND—The M-1 rifle that was replaced by the M-14. Issued to the Vietnamese early in the war.

GO-TO-HELL RAG—Towel or any large cloth worn around the neck by grunts.

GRAIL—NATO name for the shoulder-fired SA-7 surface-to-air missile.

GREASE GUN—See M-3A1.
GUARD THE RADIO—Stand by in the commo bunker and listen for messages.

GUIDELINE—NATO name for SA-2 surface-to-air missile.

GUNSHIP—Armed helicopter or cargo plane that carried weapons instead of cargo.

HE—High-explosive ammunition.

HOOTCH—Almost any shelter, from temporary to long-term.

HORN—Term referring to a specific kind of radio operations that used satellites to rebroadcast messages.

HORSE—See BISCUIT.

HOTEL THREE—Helicopter landing area at Saigon's Tan Son Nhut Airport.

HUEY—UH-1 helicopter.

IN-COUNTRY—Term used to refer to American troops operating in South Vietnam. They were all in-country.

INTELLIGENCE—Any information about enemy operations. It could include troop movements, weapons capabilities, biographies of enemy commanders and general information about terrain features. Any information that would be useful in planning a mission.

IP—

KABAR—Type of military combat knife with a sharp blade and a blood groove.

KIA—Killed In Action. (Since the U.S. wasn't engaged in a declared war, the use of the term KIA wasn't authorized. KIA came to mean enemy dead. Americans were KHA—killed in hostile action.)

KLICK—One thousand meters. A kilometer.

LIMA LIMA—Land line. Refers to telephone communications between two points on the ground.

LLDB—Luc Luong Dac Biet. The South Vietnamese Special Forces. Sometimes referred to as the Look Long, Duck Back.

LOACH—

LP—Listening post. A position outside the perimeter manned by a couple of soldiers to give advance warning of enemy activity.

LSA—Lubricant used by soldiers on their weapons to ensure that they would continue to operate properly.

LZ—Landing zone.

M-3A1—Also known as a grease gun. A .45-caliber submachine gun favored in World War II by GIs because its slow rate of fire meant that the barrel didn't rise and they didn't burn through their ammo as fast as with some other weapons.

M-14—Standard rifle of the U.S. Army, eventually replaced by the M-16. It fired the standard NATO round—7.62 mm.

M-16—Standard infantry weapon of the Vietnam War. It fired 5.56 mm ammunition.

M-79—Short-barrel shoulder-fired weapon that fired a 40 mm grenade. These could be high explosives, white phosphorus or canister.

MACV—Military Assistance Command, Vietnam, replaced MAAG in 1964.

MEDEVAC—Helicopter used to take wounded to medical facilities. Also called Dustoff.

MIA—Missing in action.

MONOPOLY MONEY—A term describing MPC handed out in lieu of regular U.S. currency.

MOS—Military Occupation Specialty. It is a job description.

MPC—Military Payment Certificates. The monopoly money used instead of real cash.

NCO—Noncommissioned officer. A noncom. A sergeant.

NCOIC—NCO in charge. The senior NCO in a unit, detachment or patrol.

NDB—Nondirectional beacon. A radio beacon that could be used for homing.

NEXT—The man who was the next to be rotated home. See SHORT. See Short-Timer, less than 30 days till leave for home.

NINETEEN—Average age of combat soldier in Vietnam, as opposed to twenty-six in World War II.

NLF—National Liberation Front. Ho Chi Minh's regime.

NOUC MAM—Foul-smelling sauce used by Vietnamese.

NVA—North Vietnamese Army. Also used to designate a soldier from North Vietnam.

P (PIASTER)—Basic monetary unit in South Vietnam, worth slightly less than a penny.

PETA-PRIME—Tarlike substance that melted in the heat of the day to become a sticky black nightmare that clung to boots, clothes and equipment. It was used to hold down dust during the dry season.

PETER PILOT—Copilot of a helicopter.

PLF—Parachute landing fall. The roll used by parachutists on landing.

POW—Prisoner of war.

PRC-10—Portable radio.

PRC-25—Portable radio, lighter than the PRC-10, which it replaced.

PULL PITCH—Term used by helicopter pilots, meaning they were going to take off.

PUNJI STAKE—Sharpened bamboo hidden to penetrate the foot, sometimes dipped in feces.

PUZZLE PALACE—Term referring to the Pentagon, because no one knew what was going on in it. Puzzle Palace East referred to MACV or USARV Headquarters in Saigon.

RINGKNOCKER—Graduate of a military academy. The term refers to the ring worn by all graduates.

RIO—

RON—Remain overnight. Term used by flight crews to indicate a flight that would last longer than a day.

RPD—Soviet light machine gun, 7.62 mm.

RTO—Radio telephone operator, the radio man of a unit.

SA-2—Surface-to-air missile fired from a fixed site. It is a radar-guided missile that is nearly thirty-five feet long.

SA-7—Surface-to-air missile that is shoulder-fired and infrared homing.

SACSA—Special Assistant for Counterinsurgency and Special Activities.

SAFE AREA—A selected area for evasion. It doesn't mean that the area is safe from the enemy, only that the terrain, location or local population make the area a good place for escape and evasion.

SAM TWO—Term referring to the SA-2 Guideline.

SAR—Search and rescue. SAR forces were the people involved in search and rescue missions.

SFOB—Special Forces Operational Base.

SHIT HOOK—Name applied by the troops to the Chinook helicopter because of all the "shit" stirred up by its massive rotors.

SHORT—Term used by everyone in Vietnam to tell all who would listen that his tour was almost over.

SHORT-TIME—GI term for a quickie.

SHORT-TIMER—Person who had been in Vietnam for nearly a year and who would be rotated back to the World soon. When his DEROS was the shortest in the unit, the person was said to be next.

SINGLE DIGIT MIDGET—Soldier with fewer than ten days left in-country.

SIX—Radio call sign for the unit commander.

SKS—Soviet-made carbine.

SMG—Submachine gun.

SOI—Signal operating instructions. The booklet that contained the call signs and radio frequencies of the units in Vietnam.

SOP—Standard operating procedure.

SPIKE TEAM—Special Forces team made up for a direct action mission.

SSB—Single side band—method of radio signal transmission.

STEEL POT—Standard U.S. Army helmet. The steel pot was the outer metal cover.

START CART—

TEAM UNIFORM OR COMPANY UNIFORM—UHF radio frequency on which the team or the company communicates. Frequencies were changed periodically in an attempt to confuse the enemy.

TDY—Temporary duty, temporary assignment.

THREE—Radio call sign of the operations officer.

THREE CORPS—The military area around Saigon. Vietnam was divided into four corps areas.

TO&E—Table of organization and equipment. A detailed listing of all the men and equipment assigned to a unit.

TOC—Tactical operations center.

TOT—Time over target, referring to the time that aircraft were supposed to be over the drop zone with parachutists, or over the target if the planes were bombers.

TRICK CHIEF—NCOIC for a shift.

TRIPLE A—Antiaircraft artillery or AAA. Anything used to shoot at airplanes and helicopters.

TWO—Radio call sign of the intelligence officer.

TWO-OH-ONE (201) FILE—Military records file that listed a soldier's qualifications, training, experience and abilities. It was passed from unit to unit so that the new commander would have some idea about the capabilities of an incoming soldier.

UMZ—Ultramilitarized zone, the name GIs gave to the DMZ (Demilitarized Zone).

UNIFORM—Refers to UHF radio. Company Uniform would be the frequency assigned to that company.

USARV—United States Army, Vietnam.

VC—Vietcong, called Victor Charlie (phonetic alphabet) or just Charlie.

VIETCONG—Contraction of Vietnam Cong San (Vietnamese Communist).

VIETCONG SAN—Vietnamese Communist. A term in use since 1956.

WHITE MICE—Term referring to the South Vietnamese military police, because they wore white helmets.

WIA—Wounded In Action.

WILLIE PETE—WP, white phosphorus, called smoke rounds. Also used as antipersonnel weapon.

WORLD—The United States.

WSO—Weapons system officer. The name given to the man who rode in the back seat of a Phantom because he was responsible for the weapons systems.

XIN LOI—Vietnamese for "sorry 'bout that."

XO—Executive officer of a unit.

ZAP—To ding, pop caps or shoot. To kill.

ZIP—Derogatory term applied to the South Vietnamese.

ZIPPO—Flamethrower.

Nile Barrabas and his soldiers have one very simple ambition: to do what the Marines can't or won't do.

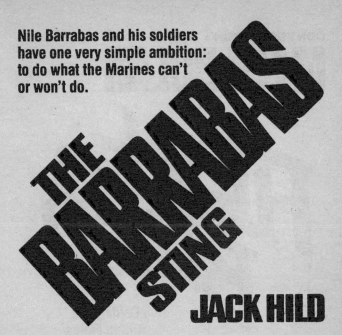

THE BARRABAS STING

JACK HILD

A former dictator, currently based in the U.S., tries to use his political and economic sway in Washington to regain power in his island home located in the South Pacific . . . and only Nile Barrabas and his men know how to stop him!

DON PENDLETON's

MACK BOLAN

California's
Killing Fields

Terror strikes innocent refugees of Southern California's Vietnamese community when they are threatened by the ruthless king
of Asia's underworld. Their one and only hope lies with Mack Bo-
lan, and when he challenges the mob, the gangland violence
rocks California.

You don't know what
NONSTOP
HIGH-VOLTAGE
ACTION
is until
you've read your
4 FREE
GOLD EAGLE
NOVELS